THE EVENT

Tori Shannon

The Event

One marriage is extinguished, another ignites.

Terry and Libby Gardner's marriage is on the rocks. He's charging hard to make partner in his law firm but finds ambition comes at a cost—his wife's fidelity. Libby feels as if her husband has abandoned her for a mistress named work and reacts by cutting him off both emotionally and sexually.

Libby is keenly aware that she's become a living cliché of Westport, Connecticut's yoga wives by fantasizing about having an affair with her in-home personal trainer, Jack Gregory, known by his female clients as *The Rock of Westport*. She's had some near misses over the years, but Jack's frequent presence in her home is becoming irresistible. Terry's decision to take a business trip in place of attending Libby's long-planned art exhibition is all the justification she needs to turn her fantasies into reality.

The Event is the debut erotic novel from Tori Shannon. By day she's a mainstream fiction writer. At night, though, the candles are lit, the wine is poured, and the cliterature is crafted as her imagination runs wild. She excels at crafting colorful characters whose struggles are real and vividly paints scenes that you can taste, smell, and feel. She knows what you like and gives it to you until you just can't take any more, and then pushes just a little bit deeper.

ISBN:1-7321846-1-5
ISBN-13:978-1-7321846-1-9

For all of the Marleys of the world who awaken those dormant desires lurking just beneath the surface

Prologue - Graduation Day

Looking back on it, I knew my marriage was as dead as a doornail well before the night last year when I decided to step out on my husband. I knew it as surely as good old Ebenezer Scrooge knew his friend Marley was dead that Christmas Eve night when his ghost visited the old penny pincher offering a chance at redemption. Coincidentally, my own chance at redemption was offered by someone named Marley—my closest friend in the world, Marley Carlin; though unlike Dickens' old miser, I didn't take my Marley's advice.

At the time, I blamed all of my marital issues on my husband, Terry. He was so goddamned driven to make partner in his law firm that I felt as if he'd abandoned me for a mistress named work. Now with The Event—which is what I call the death of my marriage—a full twelve months in the rearview mirror, I accept the fact that while my husband crafted the coffin, I hammered the nails into it. Marley also played a role—she dug the grave.

This insight into my role in the death of my marriage didn't come overnight. For the past twelve months, I've taken a series of workshops led by a self-awareness group called Personal Encounter Therapies or PET for short. The goal of PET is to bring about personal change by raising self-awareness around one's deficiencies in a certain area, often through the analysis of a failure. The death of my marriage certainly fit that criteria.

I've just completed the final workshop, but before I can graduate from the program, I have to present what I've learned about myself over the past year—kind of like how a doctoral student has to craft a dissertation before earning the designation of Ph.D. As such, I have to leave a written record of what I've learned about myself, not only for my own benefit but so that other couples can learn from my story and hopefully spot the potentially troublesome attitudes and behaviors that creep up in every marriage before it's too late.

If you are reading this, chances are you are feeling incomplete in your marriage or long-term relationship. I sincerely hope that my story will help you address issues so that you don't have to go through what I went through last year.

Before you continue reading, though, I have to warn you about something—what you are about to read is a *complete* review of what happened in my life last year and *all* of the things that led up to it. One of PET's ground rules is to be completely honest about these experiences and therefore you need to know that this is an *uncensored* account of The Event; if vivid descriptions of sexual acts are offensive to you, put this down right now and turn to a less graphic resource for help.

Also, part and parcel with PET's focus on honesty is telling one's story from multiple points of view. While Terry didn't participate in this course with me, he agreed to share his recollection of The Event to provide additional context around how our lives were turned sideways. As such, I will be sharing bits and pieces from his point of view, in his voice, throughout this work; this way, you will get his side of the story in addition to mine, and that's only fair.

I'm comfortable with the fact that, as you read this, at times you may root for me while at other times you might hate me; certainly after twelve months of investigating my own self there are things I wish I could undo because I am not proud of them—but I've exposed myself for you to see and learn from. That said, I do ask that you read this with an open mind because, if you do, you just might learn something.

Happy Reading,

Your new friend Libby

CHAPTER ONE

The Warm Summer Rain

I never wanted to be a law widow—my mother was a lawyer's wife and I saw how unhappy that made her. The constant absence of my father led her to seek extramarital attention, a fact that I certainly don't hold against her because, hey, those who live in glass houses shouldn't throw boulders. But here's the real rub, my guy wasn't even supposed to be a lawyer.

When I met him during my freshman year in college, he was a senior about to graduate at the top of his class with a degree in English and wanted nothing more than to be a writer, something that was very much in line with my bohemian ways. As the daughter of a high-powered Manhattan attorney, I tried my hardest to rebel from my father, and majoring in art at a liberal arts college in New England fit into my M.O.—so did dating a poor kid from South Florida.

After he graduated, Terry worked for a year at a large publishing house where he hunted a slush pile day and night for the proverbial needle in a haystack. He made no money—a fact that my father never let me forget. When my father realized that Terry was likely to stay in my life, dear old dad took Terry aside after dinner on Christmas Eve and encouraged him to consider a career in law.

My contempt for lawyers like my father really begs the question, why did I marry a lawyer if that's the last thing in the world I wanted? You could say that I, Libby Gardner, threw caution to the wind and convinced myself that Terry would be different, but that would be a lie. You could imagine that I'm a super-nurturing person and made it my personal mission to change him, but behind door number two there is no prize either. No, I married Terry because I was madly in love with him, and at the time, he was all I ever thought about. So yes, I did it for love. As proof, the marriage certificate was signed by the priest, the town clerk, Terry's best friend Jake and my dearest friend in the world at the time, Marley. In the beginning, our marriage was legit, there is no doubt whatever about that.

When we were first married, things were actually great. While Terry worked long hours, it didn't bother me that much because I was doing the same as an entry-level employee working in the art department of an advertising agency. While weeks were busy, we enjoyed adventurous weekends together; last-minute jaunts to the Cape were common, as were wine tasting weekends at vineyards in the Hamptons. Hell, sometimes we'd go into NY and get a hotel room just to have some hot hotel sex, but as Terry rose through the ranks of his law firm, those little adventures that keep a marriage fresh fell by the wayside.

It wasn't all bad, though. One of the positive things that happened when Terry started to ascend in his firm was that his salary jumped significantly, so that when my job as a junior art director was eliminated after my agency was sold, we could survive off of his income. That's when I started painting again.

With free time during the day to paint, I amassed quite a collection of work and started selling it out of my house to my girlfriends in our town of Westport, Connecticut. Word spread quickly about my work and my customer base reached beyond my friends. When that happened, I found that having strangers coming in and out of my house was disruptive, so I decided to open up an art gallery on Main Street in town. I'm proud to say that, for the past ten years, Gallery 39—named after its address on Main Street—has been extremely successful.

Last year I held an exhibition of my work at this gallery. The show was entitled *Love on the Rocks* and it featured a number of works depicting couples at the end stages of their relationships (that should give you a pretty good sense of where my head was at that time). I hosted the event to raise money for a charity, and guests included a who's who of Westport society; business leaders, prominent artists, and even a now disgraced Hollywood mogul were all in attendance, though there was one person who was missing—Terry. He'd decided to take a last-minute business trip the week of the exhibition and broke his promise to get back in time.

That night was the night I gave in to the devil, the night when my carnal desires overcame me and I threw myself at the guy I'd been fantasizing over for months. Never before had something so wrong felt so right, but that one act led to the end of everything.

I'm a girl who likes (okay, loves) foreplay, so before we

get to that Thursday night's main event, I've got to rewind a few days and tell you what happened the prior Sunday as that was the day that really kick-started The Event into motion. I'm going to first tell you about that day from Terry's perspective, as it's important context to have as you consider how the week unfolds. I'll warn you that this particular entry isn't for the prudish and it certainly took me aback the first time I read it, but in a significant way it also helped me understand him more.

I will be upfront and tell you that it's true what you are about to read, I did cut him off sexually and yes, I did use sex as a way of getting things I wanted—that's a trick I learned from my mother. In my defense, in our old marriage Terry held all the power. He had the big job, our lives revolved around his schedule and he wouldn't even consider having kids until he got his almighty partnership. Sex was the only power I had in our relationship—so I did what any other woman would do in that situation, I flexed my muscle.

Okay, don't say you weren't warned, but here's what he vividly recalls about the morning that put The Event into motion.

#

Here's what no one tells you about married life—after a few years, you'll have to start paying for sex. I don't mean with a professional, although I know plenty of guys who frequent illicit massage parlors and get their rocks off in champagne rooms of strip clubs. No, I mean that after some time, marital sex becomes completely transactional. My wife once promised sex every day for a month if I agreed to buy new living room furniture, but our interior designer was the only one to get lucky when I said yes.

When I approached Libby on day number two of the "month of love," she rebuffed my advance, claiming I should not have taken her seriously.

So yes, when I want sex badly enough I have to pay for it somehow, but even then we aren't talking mind-blowing, toe-curling, earth-shattering passion. Our lovemaking is scripted—one position (missionary) and any foreplay is me giving to her and never the other way around. I won't lie and say it isn't good, it is, it's just not fulfilling. I have a very active imagination and want to put it into practice, but every time I ask for something different, Libby sighs and then changes to whatever position I ask her to get in —talk about a mood killer! So, I'd settle for missionary on those rare occasions when love was in the air—when you are on the quarterly plan when it comes to the marital embrace, you take what you can get.

So that morning, like many mornings before, I took matters into my own hands. My wife was a creature of habit and always got out of bed before me to make a pot of coffee. I loved this about her for two reasons: She made great coffee, and it allowed me approximately ten minutes of Terry time before she returned to bed, coffee and bagel in hand. I'm sure she knew what I was doing as I often joked with her before she went downstairs. Our typical exchange went like this:

"Can you give me a hand with something before you go downstairs?"

"Nice try," she'd say. "The tissues are on the nightstand."

The moment she left our room that morning, I slid my hands under the sheets, put my fingers around the waistband of my briefs and tugged them downward. I'm a morning person when it comes to sex, not that I discriminate by day part, and started to gently caress myself until blood flowed from one head to the other and I was standing at attention. I then closed my eyes, took a deep breath, and relived an experience I had in college (before I met Libby).

Susan led me upstairs to her bedroom, we had to be very quiet while ascending the stairs because guys weren't allowed on the second floor of a sorority house. I'm sure we weren't the first two to break that rule and that the punishment wouldn't be that severe, but better to be safe than sorry.

I wasn't sure if we were just going to make out or do something more, but nevertheless my heart was pounding with anticipation. My question was answered when, after a passionate open-mouthed kiss, Susan started unbuckling my pants.

"You came on the dance floor, didn't you?" she said while running her fingers down my stomach in search of the evidence.

I'm embarrassed to admit it, but she's right—I did. Just minutes before entering her sorority house like a couple of cat burglars, we were at a party across the street and she and I were grinding to a Nine Inch Nails song ("Closer"). As Trent Reznor moaned, "I want to fuck you like an animal," and Susan ground herself into my pelvis, I lost control.

"Yes," I said shyly. "My whole existence is flawed."

"Good," she said with a devilish look in her eye and then told me to take off her jeans. I'd never been with someone so sexually aggressive before, I'll admit to being a bit nervous.

Once her clothes were a memory, I marveled over how good she looked. Even though her room was dark, there was enough moonlight coming in where I could make out every feature of her body: her perky breasts that were calling my name, her toned stomach that served as proof of her dedication to fitness, and her sculpturesque backside that

I just couldn't get my eyes off of—I wanted so badly to bury my face into that perfect specimen of an ass. She looked so good I had no problem resetting and was ready for her quickly after my release on the dance floor.

She instructed me to climb the ladder that led to her bed and I did so without hesitation—a horny Jack in the beanstalk—except my beanstalk got bent on one of the rungs of the ladder and I winced as I got into her bed. Would she kiss it to make it better?

I rested on my back and wasn't prepared for what was about to happen. I figured we'd kiss for a bit and make out, but before I knew it, her hips were hovering over my face and she lowered herself down onto my mouth. I'll never forget how good her essence smelled and tasted—a sumptuous feast. Sue was already excited when I started exploring her femininity with my mouth, and getting more and more excited with each flick of my tongue.

"Slow down, cowboy," she said and added, "I'm taking over from here," and started to rock her hips back and forth slowly and then increased the speed as her passion and desire reached a climax. She then dismounted my face and started kissing my lips, not at all bothered by the taste of her own sex. Yes, she was truly a unique woman.

She then started kissing my neck and stuck her tongue in my ear— a sensation I can't explain but feels like ecstasy. Continuing to work her way south, she kissed my nipples and slid her tongue down my stomach until she couldn't go any farther without running into my excitement, which, by this point, was throbbing with desire, but she took a detour and teased me for a bit. To this day I'm not even sure what she did or how she did it, but I can tell you this, no one has made me feel that way since. I've never done heroin, but if it is anything remotely like the sensation she gave me late that night, I have no problem understanding why use of that drug is on the rise. I recall seeing stars and letting out a moan that was, most likely, heard by her sisters in the next room over, anyone with a pulse on campus, and perhaps by humans all the way in Missouri where her sorority's headquarters were located.

Knowing what she had just put me through, she teased me with her tongue and took me into her mouth—shallow at first and then as deep as she could. I had girls who had given me oral before, and I'm aware that many do it not out of desire but out of a sense of obligation, but this was on another level. She was so in tune with my desire it was almost like she was getting as much pleasure giving as I was receiving.

The desire was quickly coming to a boiling point and I told her that I was about to finish, thinking she would take me out of her mouth and complete the act with her hand. I was shocked when my admission caused her to move her head up and down with an increasing amount of speed. Involuntary reflexes took over and I had reached the point of no return. As I pulsated in her mouth, she herself seemed to release with delight.

"You can't stay here," she said when the act was over.

I tried kissing her nipples, which I had largely ignored since she mounted my face so quickly before, but that didn't change the fact that I wasn't supposed to be in her room when the sun came up, and by now morning was breaking.

We both got dressed and she led me downstairs, once again tiptoeing so we didn't arouse the suspicion of her sisters. We kissed again at the back door and said our final goodbyes.

After working myself over for ten minutes that morning, I wasn't ready to release. I wanted more time with my memories of Susan but knew that Libby would be back upstairs at any moment, coffee cup in hand and a strong desire to watch Sunday morning news programs.

"I'm going to have my coffee down here this morning," her voice called from downstairs. "Want to join me?"

"I just need a few more minutes and then I'll be down," I said from the bedroom. I remember feeling a twinge of guilt when I said this as my mind had been preoccupied by another woman since my wife had gone downstairs.

"Suit yourself, but I can't promise you'll get any when you come down."

"I knew I wasn't getting any anyway," I muttered.

At that moment, I couldn't have cared less about coffee —I had a throbbing problem that needed to be solved— but not before imagining another fantasy starring Susan. I closed my eyes and got lost in thought.

We hooked up two other times that semester: once in the parlor room of her sorority house—a particularly exciting session given any of her sisters could have walked in on us—and once in my off-campus apartment after sharing a joint and a bottle of wine. We never had sex though—a fact that I was increasingly regretting.

When I was out of real memories, I started to think about what slipping inside her would feel like. I imagined my chest pressed against hers and our hearts beating together, rapidly. As I dreamt this up I could actually feel the thump, thump, thump of our hearts in synchronization. I dreamed about how our hips would move in synch and how we'd stare into each other's eyes until we climaxed together, and then finally collapse with exhaustion.

As I had these thoughts, I felt that unmistakable reflex start to pulsate in my hand and soon after I felt something like warm summer rain fall onto my stomach and chest. It was the strongest orgasm I had in weeks and the aforementioned Kleenex wasn't going to cut it. I got out of bed and headed towards the bathroom and turned on the shower.

#

I'll admit it, that morning I knew exactly what Terry was

doing in our bedroom; I'm not an idiot. I knew he was a horny guy (that's redundant, isn't it?). And yes, it was shocking to read such a vivid fantasy about another woman, but this served as a reminder that, had we been open to speaking with each other about what we wanted sexually, a lot of heartache could have been avoided.

At that time, we'd been a couple for almost twenty years and I had no idea that he would have been interested in my taking control in the bedroom—I just assumed he wanted to be in charge. He, on the other hand, had no idea that I wanted to be told, not asked, what to do— which explained why I sighed when he'd ask to change positions. I wanted an alpha, and alphas don't ask.

CHAPTER TWO

My Near Miss

While Terry was playing a scene from his college "go-to" reel, I exchanged texts with my closest friend at the time, Marley. I saved that exchange so what you are about to read is accurate, captured forever on the servers of AT&T Wireless.

Marley and I had been best friends since grade school. We held no secrets from each other—I knew about all her sexually dominant ways as well as everything she did to her submissive boyfriends. In a world where women are still skittish about revealing their sexual desires, Marley was one of the few who wasn't afraid to not only ask for what she wanted, but take it. If she were a guy, I'd be totally into her. She once told me that I'm a stereotypical sub and encouraged me to tell Terry to be more dominant —advice I didn't take at the time because it was my belief that men should just know how to be dominant. That was a big mistake on my part.

Marley also knew everything about me. I confided in her my relationship woes with Terry and she knew that I'd all but cut him off in the bedroom. I'll never forget her reaction when I told her that news. "Why punish yourself, chica?"

It was a fair question, I love sex just like everyone else, but while I was denying myself intercourse with Terry, it felt good to hold at least some power in my relationship.

Here was our text exchange that morning:

L: You up?

M: What's up chica?

Marley isn't a Latina, she just talks like one. In fact, she's a fair-skinned redhead who looks to be right off the boat from the Emerald Isle. Like all redheads I know, the woman has a fiery, take-charge personality that scares some men but is enthralling to others.

L: Just having coffee, solo. Terry is in the shower.

M: Why don't you join him? Make it a Sunday funday, LOL.

L: I'm not in the mood.

M: Girl, you are never in the mood for that man. You gotta be careful because one day that patient little hot piece of ass you call a husband is going to wind up between another woman's legs.

L: He'd never do that.

I believed what I said—if taking my husband for granted were an Olympic sport, I would have earned a gold medal. In my mind, Terry may not have been getting what he wanted from me, but I knew he truly loved me and couldn't imagine him having the nerve to cheat. I was the one with the near miss, and Marley never let me forget it.

M: Don't be so sure. You almost strayed, he will too if you give him enough time. Dry spells go against their nature, and his seeing your hot little body all the time must be driving him crazy. Mark my words chica, the minute he has an opportunity, he'll stray, just like you almost did that weekend in New York.

I'm going to pause here and tell you about my near miss because it will help you understand the thin ice I had been skating on in the time leading up to The Event.

A few months before that fateful Thursday, Marley and I spent a girls' weekend in New York. I was feeling kind of bummed about where things stood with Terry and she thought a few nights of dancing were exactly what I needed to get my mind off of things.

Marley wasn't tied down by anybody—she was very open about her polyamorous lifestyle with every guy she dated and when we went out it was clear that I was her wing woman—someone to "babysit" any friend who was tagging along with a guy she was interested in. On our first night in NY we wound up at a trendy club called Vertigo and she caught the eyes of a pair of identical twins. One smile from Marley was all it took to get them walking in our direction and the next thing you know, we had two free drinks.

Their names were Michael and James, both claimed to be actors, which was pretty likely given they had flawless faces, strong-looking builds, and haircuts that betrayed the fact that neither went to a barber for a cut—stylists all the way. The only discernible difference between them was the fact that Michael parted his hair from right to left where James wore his left to right. Marley wasted no time getting James on the dance floor, leaving me alone to entertain Michael. Of course, I'm making this sound a lot worse than it was because, well, he was really hot; it's just that I wasn't there to hook up. How could I be? I was married!

No, I wasn't looking for a quick Band-Aid for my marital woes, but there is something about being in a dance club that is very sensual: the people dancing and grinding on each other, the thump, thump, thump of the beat, and the atmosphere of sexual tension as bodies move together in rhythm. Being in that club and then staring into the eyes of the incredibly handsome man in front of me flicked a switch inside me that hadn't been turned on in a long time.

"Would you like to dance?" Michael asked while he stood up and extended his hand with all the confidence of a guy who rarely heard the word no.

I then had an angel on one shoulder, devil on the other moment. In the close calls I had in the past I always listened to the angel, but there was something different going on that night. The angel whispered "no," but the devil on the other shoulder shouted "YES," and I decided it just might be time to give the devil his due.

"As a matter of fact, I would," I replied and reached for his hand. He led me onto the floor where the DJ was playing something with a strong bass beat that went straight up my legs and tingled me just below the waist. I knew I was in trouble when I had a hard time breaking contact with those crisp, blue eyes.

I didn't intend for my time on the dance floor to lead to an indiscretion, but then I remembered what my grandmother always told me about good intentions, the road to hell is paved with them.

I broke contact with Michael's eyes to look around for Marley and saw that she was making out with James on the dance floor. How long had it been since I'd gotten lost in a kiss so intense? Five years? Ten? Michael must have noticed me staring at them and took the wanting look I was wearing on my face as an opportunity to pull me close and go for my lips. I was caught off guard and resisted at first, but he pushed forward and didn't relent; with the music blaring, and all those bodies bumping and grinding all around me, I gave in and opened my mouth.

That man knew how to kiss! He didn't rush in with his tongue the way some guys do—he was patient, softly kissing my upper lip at first and then spending some time kissing the lower one, all the while lightly grazing them with his tongue. It wasn't until he grabbed my face in his hands that our tongues touched and I could feel the butterflies that had been fluttering around in my stomach work their way southward until they came to flutter between my legs.

Sensing my resistance was down, Michael walked me to a corner and pulled me close. His hands ran down my back until they rested on my hips—and then went lower. He ever so gently squeezed me with his hands as if my ass was the most delicate thing in the world to him and he was afraid of breaking it—I could tell this was a man who took his time. As he leaned into me, I could feel the excitement in his pants pressing up against my stomach, leaving no question that I was turning him on as much as he was starting me up.

"How about we go someplace quiet?" He took my smile as a yes and pulled me by the hand through the club until we came to one of Vertigo's unisex bathrooms. With my heart racing a thousand beats per minute, I followed him in and luckily there was no one else inside. He led me to a stall, the glass in which immediately fogged up when he locked the door. There were walls from the floor to the ceiling and no one would be able to tell what was going on inside.

He leaned in for a kiss and I willingly gave in to the desire that was burning inside me; there was no trace of the angel left on my shoulder, only the devil remained poking at me with his pitchfork (or was that Michael's excitement?). While I could say it was his good looks that were making my heart race, it was actually the fact that, for the first time in forever, I was with a guy who wasn't afraid to take charge; his confidence was more of an aphrodisiac than that movie-star face.

He diverted his attention to my neck, which he kissed with the ferocity of a vampire who has not feasted in weeks, pausing only to suck in my flesh and nibble it with his teeth. While his mouth was working above my waist, his hands dropped below and he started hiking up my dress ever so slightly until I felt his strong hands cup my ass. I gave out a slight moan as the sensation of his skin on mine was electrifying. My response encouraged him to spin me around so that his excitement, still trapped in his pants, was pressing up against the line of my thong. He slid his hands slowly up my body and cupped my breasts while working the back of my neck with his mouth—it had been so long since I'd felt a fraction of this attention and the fluttering between my legs was becoming unbearable. I reached my left hand around my body to caress his excitement and used my right hand to guide his below my waist and under my skirt until his fingers rested on that spot between my legs which was starting to drip with excitement.

Just as he lifted the side of my thong aside with his finger, I started to unzip his pants with my hand. Just as his finger was feeling how excited I was, I heard the bathroom door swing open and my name being called.

"Libby, are you in here?"

"Shhh," Michael whispered into my ear and placed a finger to my lips, the same one he'd been using to explore me. Since he'd been giving me all the attention, I decided to wrap my lips around that finger and take it into my mouth. His excitement had clearly dwindled since the bathroom door swung open, but my mimicking oral on his glistening middle finger changed all that and I could feel his excitement pressing up against me once again.

"Goddammit, Libby, where the fuck are you?" I heard through the stall.

"What are you doing?" a male's voice asked.

"Calling her," Marley replied.

I had custom ring tones for the important people in my life. When Terry called, my phone would announce, "You can't handle the truth," as it's a quote from his favorite movie, *A Few Good Men*. While my dad encouraged him to go into law school, Tom Cruise, Jack Nicholson, and that lovable little Kevin Pollak also painted a picture for Terry that being a lawyer could be glamorous. At that moment, though, while standing in a bathroom stall with Michael the actor, whose finger I was blowing in my mouth, my phone started playing Abba's "Dancing Queen."

"Shit," I said and then opened the door.

"Libby, you are coming with me now!"

"Hey!" Michael protested, but Marley got in between us.

"She's married, asshole."

She pulled me out of the bathroom and we left the club for our hotel.

The fact that my phone had started to vibrate in my hands took me out of my daydream and brought me back to my Sunday morning exchange with Marley (though I had to reread her last text to remember exactly where we left off).

L: He's not aggressive enough with me. He never says what he wants. If he wants me, he's got to take me.

M: I'll have more to say on that later chica, assuming we are still on for drinks at 2.

L: Been looking forward to that all week. The Duck?

The Black Duck Cafe is Westport, Connecticut's local dive. The bar was built in an old house boat and rested on the shores of the Saugatuck River. While women in my socioeconomic class tended to frequent the town's more upscale restaurants, every now and then I reverted back to my rebellious ways and patronized the Black Quack, as I called it. Oh, and the Sunday bartender at the Duck was beyond hot. Given my self-imposed exile from penetrative sex, I enjoyed a little eye candy for my own fantasy reel.

M: Si chica. See you then.

I placed my phone face down and heard Terry coming down the stairs.

"You weren't kidding about the coffee," Terry said while pouring the remainder of the pot into a mug. He then walked over to the microwave to heat it up.

"You snooze, you lose, Terry Gardner."

I remember he looked at me with a smirk. He was dressed in golf clothes, like he was every Sunday, and that smirk, combined with the outfit, made me want to slap him. The funny thing was, I used to love that smirk, but something about it that morning was distasteful.

"I just want to remind you I'm heading out for drinks

with Marley at two. What's on tap for you today?" As if I didn't know.

"Going to play eighteen with Preston at the club."

Preston Cantor was a senior partner at Terry's law firm and technically his boss. Terry knew he was close to making partner and devoted an increasing amount of his weekend time schmoozing with the firm's management, a move considered necessary to get the nod from the higher-ups to join their ranks.

"Hey, why don't you and Marley meet us there and we can all have drinks together? We'll likely be finishing up around then."

Country clubs represented everything an artistic soul like me hated about the privileged class and the thought of giving up my afternoon at the Duck (and the eye candy that was the bartender) to head to his club made my stomach turn. I wore that feeling on my face.

"Jesus, Libby, tell me how you really feel."

"It's important for you to have this time with Prescott…"

"Preston," Terry corrected me.

"Whatever." I know that it bothered my husband that I didn't take any interest in his career, but it bothered me that all he cared about was making partner in his firm. If he put half the effort into me as he did into his career, I might have had the emotional satisfaction to open myself up to him physically. I simply wanted to feel wanted by my husband, but didn't. All I felt was empty—at least that was something we had in common.

"I don't want to get in the way. I'll see you tonight for dinner."

Terry walked towards the door, and then I remembered

that my husband might need a reminder about my art exhibition that coming Thursday.

"Oh, do you need me to get you a new tie for Thursday night?"

"I'm going to wear the pink one you got me for Christmas."

I'll admit to being surprised that he didn't ask what's going on Thursday night.

"If you change your mind, text me before one."

He left without kissing goodbye and I went upstairs to draw a bath. Terry had his release and I was about to have mine.

CHAPTER THREE

A Mile High in Denver

While I had that near miss in New York a few months before The Event, it turned out Terry had a near miss of his own. Marley was right, using sex as a tool for getting what I wanted had been taking a toll on him—and that led to an almost indiscretion in the mile-high city.

He shared that with me after our marriage fell apart last year and I'm including his story here to detail where his mind was at. Note, Terry, of course, changed the name of the woman he met in Denver, but I'm not sold on the name he used. You'll see why in a minute.

#

Nothing made me feel more alive than a drive along the windy back roads of Westport with the top of my Porsche down. The car was a gift to myself after the prior year's bonus—eighty-hour work weeks had started to pay off and I heard through the firm's rumor mill that I was on a short list of senior associates to make partner by the end of the year. I allowed myself a smile but was brought back to reality by the ringing in my ear.

I looked at the digital display on my dashboard to see who was calling and dreamed it was Libby telling me that she changed her mind about lunch and was going to meet me at the club after all, though I knew in my heart that wasn't likely as my country club was her kryptonite. The name on the screen was that of Robbie Morgan, my closest friend on the planet who never matured past the age of nineteen.

"Please tell me you aren't in prison and need bail, I'm on my way to the club."

Robbie and I ribbed each other incessantly; the fact is, I had bailed him out of jail on more than one occasion—and would certainly do it again if asked.

"Well, look at you, Mr. Fancy Pants. No, I'm not in the hoosegow, though I am into prison porn. Last night I watched this movie called *Sex in the Slammer*…"

"I don't need the details." I had to cut him off before he gave me a scene-by-scene description.

"What day are you going on?"

He wanted to know how long it had been since I'd last slept with Libby. Why he was fascinated by my love life, or lack thereof, I couldn't tell you.

"Tomorrow we enter triple digits."

"What the fucking fuck, man? That's like over three months without any—how are you not climbing the walls?"

"I just deal with it. Is there some reason you are calling, aside from probing into my non-existent sex life, that is?"

"Yeah, you fucker. You never told me about your trip to Denver. You made it sound like you almost got lucky."

Right then and there I realized that drunk texting Robbie while attending a cocktail party at a conference wasn't a great idea. Divulging that I was flirting with a woman opened a window for my friend's overly active imagination, one that wouldn't be shut until I told him all of the details.

"Nothing happened."

"Fuck you nothing happened!" Robbie said. "Your specific words were, 'holy fuck, Robbie, I might actually cheat on Libby tonight,' and then our exchange went dead. Who the fuck teases someone like that and then doesn't provide details? What kind of monster are you?"

"There's nothing much to tell," I said. It was true, the flirting went nowhere, but it wasn't for lack of trying.

"Details, or I send our texts to Libby." It was a threat, and because I knew him better than anyone, I fully understood that Robbie would follow through with it until I spilled the beans.

"You are a son of a bitch, you know that?"

"I haven't got all day, they only allow us ten minutes on the phone in lock-up."

I pulled my car to the side of the road, put the top back up to eliminate the possibility that someone would overhear my confession, and then recounted what happened last week in Colorado.

I was representing my firm at a conference exploring the results of Colorado's choice to legalize marijuana for recreational use. My state of Connecticut had some significant budget issues given that our esteemed governor had singlehandedly run the economy of one of the wealthiest states in the country right into the ground. While he was looking to building new casinos and adding tolls along our highways to put a Band-Aid on our budget crisis, there was a group of us in the legal community who were advocating for making cannabis legal in Connecticut and placing a high sales tax on it. My firm sent me to

Colorado to learn how it's worked out there.

After the last session on the final day of the conference, I joined some other attendees for drinks in the bar, and that's where I met Violet. I'd seen her throughout the conference—I'd had to have been blind to have missed her; she had red hair like Libby's friend Marley that flowed to the center of her back and wore form-fitting suits throughout the conference. Dark, thick-framed glasses capped off her look—on anyone else they would have looked goofy, but on Violet they screamed Your book is overdue and I'm going to make you pay with your penis.

As the crowd at the bar dispersed, I noticed her hanging around. I was having this internal debate about whether or not I should move in closer when, to my relief, she made the first move and started walking towards me. I immediately put my left hand into my pocket and flicked off my wedding ring—an action I had done numerous times before in anticipation of finally getting up the nerve to flirt with a woman in a bar.

She extended her hand, looked me directly in the eye, and said, "My name is Violet Beauchamp from Chicago. I thought your question about how to open up capital markets for entrepreneurs in this space was super smart."

Growing cannabis had traditionally been something that was done by small, underground growers in the US and, of course, the cartels in Mexico and other places. Legalization of the crop would require large-scale production and that meant entrepreneurs in the space would require access to capital. With the stigma around pot that has existed for the past century, I wondered how future growers would get access to capital—a resource largely controlled by more conservative types. My question led to a lot of discussion and I had been receiving compliments on it all evening, but none from someone as striking as Violet Beauchamp from Chicago.

"It's an important consideration," I said. "I'm happy to discuss it

more with you." As the words left my body, my heart started to beat faster and I could feel my body temperature rise. Was that sweat dripping down my back?

"I'd like that," she said. Her green eyes were mesmerizing; there was something about the combination of her red hair and green eyes that made me think of Christmas—and I wanted nothing more than to unwrap her as the greatest present Denver could give me.

"Don't you think it's much too loud here?" she added.

Loud? It wasn't loud at all. The bar had started to empty out and there was only a handful of people left. I looked around and was about to question her observation when a light bulb went off in my head—she didn't want to talk about capital markets for cannabis entrepreneurs. She didn't want to talk about anything, she wanted to be alone with me. The thought sent a shiver down my spine and my mouth became dry instantly at that realization.

"Now that you mention it," I managed to say, "it is a little loud in here. Stuffy too."

"I'm glad you agree," she said. "Go to the bar and get us two more glasses of wine and let's get out of here. I'm just going to freshen up for a minute."

She left for the ladies' room and I made a beeline for the bar to get two more glasses of vino. I tapped out a note to Robbie while I was waiting.

Violet came back and downed her wine as if it was water. I did the same and she took my hand and led me out of the bar.

While we walked towards the elevators, the guilt started to creep in. My wife may have cut me off sexually, but she was still someone I had made a promise to, a commitment before God, our families, our friends, and yes, even Robbie. Was I really about to throw it all away on a one-night stand in Colorado? The bing of the elevator brought my thoughts rushing back to reality and Violet leaned in and whispered into my ear, "Second thoughts?"

She smelled so good. That perfume, eau du transgression, had me hypnotized. I entered the elevator knowing that I might be about to make the biggest mistake of my life, but as she grabbed me by the wrist and pulled me in, those cares fell away.

"What floor?" she asked. Apparently, we were going to my room.

"Thirteen," I said. She pushed the button and then turned around and kissed me with more passion than I had experienced in each of the last fifteen years of my marriage combined. She then wrapped her arms around my neck and jumped on me so that I had to hold her bottom with both of my hands to maintain my balance. My knees started to tremble on the ride upward—just when I thought that my legs would give out, the elevator binged, came to a stop, and we got off. Saved by the bell.

"Number?" Violet asked.

"1321," I said, and she made a left out of the elevator, all the while tugging me by the wrist.

As we stood in front of my door, I reached into my left pocket and pulled out my room key, but along with the key came my wedding band, which made a clinking sound when it hit the door. Violet and I both looked down at the same time and once she realized what had fallen out of my pocket, the passion in the air evaporated like steam off of boiling water.

"Are you fucking married?"

"Listen, it's complicated."

"Arghhhh!" she screamed while walking away from my door. "I can't fuck a married guy, I'm not some sort of home wrecker."

"Look, my marriage is sexless…"

She cut me off. "But it's still a marriage. You fucking guys are all the same."

"Wait a minute," I started to mount my defense, "you approached me."

"That's right, and you weren't wearing a wedding ring at the time.

Do you think I would have come on to you if I knew you were married? I may be an independent woman, but I'm not going to be someone's other woman."

As the blood started coming back to my brain from parts farther south, I started to not only sympathize with what Violet was saying, but felt increasingly guilty about what had happened from the time we met in the bar to where we were right now.

"I'm sorry."

"Yeah, well, I'm sorry too," Violet said and then jumped in the elevator, leaving me alone in front of my door on the thirteenth floor.

"Rookie mistake," Robbie said. "You should never have had your ring on you at that conference at all."

"Yeah, well, I didn't go there with the intention of cheating on my wife."

"Yeah, well, I bet you didn't intend on being in a sexless marriage either."

I hate it when he mimics me. I hate it more when he has a point.

"Why do you suppose she's so frigid towards you anyway? It's not like you are a bad-looking dude. Plus, you've got a killer career. That combination should make you a magnet for her libido. Libby libido, hey, that's funny."

It's a valid question, one that I have asked myself frequently over the years. While Libby and I never went at it with the ferocity of a couple of porn stars, our lovemaking was at least somewhat regular in the early stages of our relationship. As our relationship matured, it started to level off—but didn't that happen to everyone? The truth is, at the time, I didn't know how much my focus on my career impacted my wife, I thought she had just fallen out of love with me.

"Look, I'm going to be late for my tee time. Want to grab drinks next Friday?"

"Can't," Robbie said. "I'm washing my hair, but it should be dry by Saturday."

I laughed at this as Robbie has been bald since high school.

"Friday it is."

The line went dead and I drove off toward the club where I'd spend the next five hours playing the game I loved, not golf—how to climb the corporate ladder.

#

So, okay, I'm not the only bad guy here. He had a near miss as well and I'd be a hypocrite for not understanding what brought him to that point. This isn't to say I wasn't pissed or even hurt about his admission, but over time I did come to understand it. But just like with my time with Michael on the dance floor at that club in New York, his time with Violet was just a close call. We were both batting zero for one in the adultery department, but clearly it wasn't for lack of trying.

In the spirit of sharing the full picture of The Event with you, I'm going to share another perspective from that Sunday morning as it will be important for you to get to know Marley a little better since, as you will see, she has a starring role in the death of my marriage.

CHAPTER FOUR

Under the Table and Dreaming

Marley only admitted what you are about to read after everything went down last year. It was part of our healing process and, while things have never been the same between us, my understanding of where her head was at during that period in our lives gave me the perspective I needed to fully process what happened between us; and by us, I mean Marley, Terry, and me.

She admitted that when we were texting back and forth on Sunday morning she was actually situated underneath the table that one of her boyfriends was lying on face down. The table had a hole in it about three quarters of the way down and critical parts of her guy's anatomy had fallen victim to gravity and were hanging through it. Marley's a total Dominant in the bedroom and got off on "torturing" guys as much as she did by having sex with them. Some people go to church on Sunday mornings— Marley engages in S&M. To each their own.

She'd been teasing her guy with a feather just before my text came in but stopped what she was doing to engage in the exchange with me—you might not think this visual is an important part of the story, but it does paint a picture of what Marley is into, which is an important thing to keep in mind as the events of that week unfold.

"Did you forget about me, Goddess?" the man's voice called from the other side of the table. Marley made all of her submissives refer to her as Goddess. She in turn called them sub.

"You will speak only when spoken to, sub!" Marley commanded and then punished him with a slap to those very tender parts of his manhood, which at that moment were hanging through the hole in the table.

"Ughhhh," he said and then kept quiet for fear of another reprisal. Thankfully for him, our text exchange wasn't that long.

After our exchange, Marley was angry with me for the way I'd been treating Terry— a fact that encouraged her to put a little extra pepper on the slap to her guy's gonads. To understand why Marley was mad with me, you should know that she'd secretly had a thing for Terry since the day we met him.

She and I were both first year art students at Connecticut University when Terry showed up as the male model in our figure drawing class. In my head I can still hear the sound of the entire class's gasp after Terry removed his robe and stood in front of the class naked— put simply, his body was as if a Greek sculptor chiseled it. On top of that, he was exceptionally gifted in the penis department. I'm not going to lie, size matters, ladies.

Shortly after his robe hit the floor, Marley turned to me and said, "I'd fuck him for days." She wasn't one to mince her words and the blank look in her eyes she had while she stared at Terry's anatomy made it clear to me that she was imagining riding him like a horse in that perverted little mind of hers. Last year she admitted the fact that I wasn't taking advantage of such a wonderful feat of nature made her that much more upset with me.

Back in college, Terry was a starving artist type. He could only afford to go to school on scholarship and would do anything to make a few extra bucks, including being a nude model for a figure drawing art class. The fact that we came from such different backgrounds was a real turn-on for me—at the time I'd do anything to rebel against my privileged background and pursuing a member of what my father would call the lower class certainly fit the bill.

While Marley's mind went right to jumping Terry's bones, mine went directly to wondering what was going on behind those beautiful hazel eyes of his. What was this handsome and muscular man, so comfortable with himself that he'd disrobe in front of a class full of strangers, all about? He must have been feeling the vibe I was putting out because after class he made a beeline for me. I now know of the jealousy Marley felt when he and I became an item, but at the time I didn't think anything of it.

I don't blame her for being attracted to Terry, I mean, he was hot at the time and, if I'm being honest, while I hated the fact that he became an ambitious asshole, age had treated him very kindly. Women, Marley included, found him attractive.

She told me that she'd been reflecting on her feelings for Terry, my near miss with infidelity in New York, and the fact that I'd cut him off as she tortured the submissive man lying on the table above her.

With the vitriol of an angry preacher she proclaimed, "You've gone soft on me, sub. What are we going to do about that?" Marley took it as an insult that a guy would have lost an erection in her presence.

"Whatever you want, Goddess."

This poor guy was about to have an experience he'd never forget—and to think, according to Marley, he was an aggressive, alpha-type trader at a successful hedge fund. It just goes to show that you never assume what anyone is into.

Marley, stewing about me, said, "I want you to tell me why people can't be honest with each other."

Marley told me that, as she spoke those words, she also grabbed that aforementioned most tender of areas with her hand.

"Do you have an answer?"

"Yes, Goddess. I guess some people are afraid of the reaction they will get if they tell the truth." I think it's fair to say he believed every word he just said.

Marley told me at this point she started stroking her sub faster and faster.

"Goddess, that feels so…"

Before the guy could mutter the word good, Marley, being the Dom that she is, squeezed her hand into a fist.

"Arghhhhh," her sub squeaked and then started to concentrate on his breathing to take his mind off the pain.

Marley then released the grasp she had on her sub. "What are people afraid of?" she asked while she teased him ever so gently with the tips of her fingers to build his excitement once again.

"Disappointing or hurting another person, Goddess."

Sensing her sub was building to a climax she gave her

hand a rest—and Marley says I'm cruel.

"Doesn't lying lead to disappointment and hurt feelings?"

"Only if the other person finds out, Goddess."

When Marley recounted this story for me, she told me how, upon hearing this response, she started to gently blow on her sub as a way of torturing him a little more. She loves to be in control; this was what he signed up for after all.

"So it's okay to lie because you are sparing someone you might love from being disappointed?" As she asked this, she took him in her hand again and began to squeeze.

"No, Goddess!" her guy blurted out with hopes that this would be the right answer. Apparently, it was, because Marley's hand relaxed and went to gently rubbing his unit, which was by then, I could imagine, a dark shade of purple.

"Lying is never right, Goddess. People who love and respect each other should always be truthful with one another, even if the truth hurts."

This response is precisely why I am going through the trouble of telling you this story about Marley and her sub —it is one of the core lessons I learned last year—people who love and respect each other should always be open and truthful, even if truth hurts.

I loved my husband but didn't respect him, and because of that I couldn't be honest with him about how I was feeling in our marriage—and that led me into the arms of another.

CHAPTER FIVE

A Pearl Of Great Price

This brings me to the fantasy I had that morning while soaking in my bathtub. When we were looking at houses before we got married, I knew the house we bought was right for me not because of the chef's kitchen or wine cellar, but because of the master bathroom complete with jacuzzi tub with jets that pulsate water from multiple directions.

A year ago, I would never have shared my fantasies with another person as, truthfully, I wasn't very in tune with my own sexuality. I've since learned that being true to myself and what I want is the first step in having a fulfilling sexual relationship with another person.

My sex coach, yes, that's a real thing, has helped me rewire my brain so that I no longer subconsciously view sex as something to be ashamed of, but something to value and embrace. She argues that we were formed from sex and that sex should flow through us fluidly. I want to share with you the uncensored fantasy I had that morning because it is important context for what happened the night of my art exhibition.

As the bathtub filled up with warm water, I let the bathrobe I was wearing slide down to the floor. The mirror had not yet fogged up from the steam coming from the tub and I remember staring at my naked body, trying hard not to be overly critical. At 39, I still had the flat stomach I worked so hard to achieve through personal training sessions, adhering to a strict diet and, of course, Pilates (the fact that we didn't have kids didn't hurt either). I remember thinking that my full B-cups were as perky as they were in my twenties, but still cupped them with my hands and pushed them north to see how they might look with a lift. At the risk of sounding like a braggart, I looked damn good.

If Terry were still home that morning, he'd likely try to sneak a peek at me in front of the mirror but would not be aggressive enough to give me what I really wanted—to come up from behind me, caress my chest, hold me tight and press himself against me—at the time he was too polite of a lover. Lest you think I'm some submissive chick who needs a man to control her, I can assure you that I'm not—I just crave raw masculinity from time to time and that morning I wanted to be wanted.

When the tub was half full, I slid in and positioned myself under the faucet so the warm water rushing out of it dripped over the center of my femininity—the weight of the falling warm water gave me such a rush of excitement that it pained me to turn off the faucet to prevent my bathroom from flooding.

With the water off, I switched on the jets to bring the jacuzzi to life and then grabbed the waterproof toy I stashed in the tub. With the vibrations of the water tickling every part of my body, I slid my hand downward until it rested on top of the heart of my sex. After a little teasing, I turned my toy clockwise to bring it to life and thought about Jack, my in-home trainer who came highly recommended by Westport's other law widows.

There's always something uniquely erotic about doing this in a bathtub—the weightlessness of being in the water gave me the sensation that was like floating in space, and at that time I floated towards a fantasy that I longed to make a reality. I closed my eyes and was no longer in my tub—I was in my home gym, and that's where this fantasy begins.

#

Jack tells me to take my shoes off and position myself face down on the massage table he stretches me on after our workouts.

"I'm going to start with a brief massage before we stretch. I worked you hard today and you need to get rid of some built-up lactic acid."

"Rub away," I say. Having Jack tell me what to do gets me excited—my husband is a polite lover and certainly doesn't give commands; I like being told what to do.

Jack doesn't start at the calves but uses each of his hands to lightly caress the arches of my feet—while this tickles a bit, it's not an altogether unpleasant sensation. He applies some oil to his hands and then rubs his thumbs from the balls of my feet to my heels and then pays a little attention to my ankles.

"This might hurt a bit," he warns as he slides his hands up to my calves. "Tell me if the pressure is too much."

"Hurt me," I mutter under my breath.

"What did you say?"

"Sorry," I speak up. "I just said okay."

Jack then takes the bottle of oil and lets some drip onto my calves

—the sensation is heavenly.

Once again, using his thumbs, he applies light pressure at first and gradually goes deeper.

"I want you to breathe deeply with me," he says and then inhales. I do the same until we are breathing in rhythm with one another. I feel the connection we are building start to intensify.

As I let my mind wander, I imagine that he can't help but look up towards where my shorts end just below my bottom. During our first workouts, I wore yoga pants, but in the sessions that have passed, I replaced my Lululemons with shorts that seemed to get increasingly skimpier with every passing session.

I don't care that Jack can clearly see the lines of my thong under my shorts. I imagine that as his eyes focus on those lines, his hands make their way past my calves and onto my hamstrings.

"I'm going to start stretching you out in a minute, but your hamstrings are really tight. Do you mind if I pay some attention to them?"

His hands slide up my legs and my heartbeat rises—approaching the point where it was during our workout.

"They are always that way after a workout," I say, wondering how I even got the words out as my mouth has gone bone dry.

Jack moves over to the right side of the table and uses both of his hands to start rubbing my right hamstring. He starts just below the knee and gradually makes his way up to the fold of my cheek, which I know is peeking through my shorts. As he does so, I let out a groan —not of pain but of pleasure.

Before walking to the left side of the table, Jack gives one more long, flowing stroke up my leg, once again starting just above the knee before working his way upward. This time, though, he applies only very light pressure and goes a little farther than the last time, slightly grazing my inner thigh—I let out a slight moan.

He walks over to the left side of the table and repeats the process, *going from light to firm and then down to very light pressure. As he makes his way upwards during his last stroke, I part my legs slightly —an invitation. I don't care that he can see the excitement evident between my legs.*

"How do your glutes feel?"

"My what?" I ask—I was in a daze and not thinking clearly.

Jack playfully places his hands on my butt. "Is your ass tight?"

"Very," I moan.

He walks around to the head of the table and places his hands at the base of my neck and runs them down my back in a long, flowing motion before cupping my cheeks in his hands. I now want him so bad I can taste it.

"They are really tight." Jack bends down and whispers into my ears. He's driving me crazy and I know he knows it.

"Make them un-tight," I say.

"It will be easier if you remove your shorts."

I become short of breath as I consider what I'm about to do. With my husband physically and emotionally absent over the past few years, I give in to desire.

"I don't want to turn around. Take them off for me." I want nothing more than for Jack to take charge. He gently places his fingers underneath the waistband of my shorts and pushes them downward, exposing me. He then walks from one end of the table to the other to remove them completely from my ankles.

After freeing me from my shorts, Jack returns to the head of the table and reaches under my sport top and pulls it upward until I am bare except for the black thong, which I suppose helps him leave something to imagination.

He then takes his bottle of oil, turns it upside down, and lets it drip over my cheeks, up my back and onto the base of my neck. With long, flowing motions, he massages my shoulders and back and then cups my bottom in his hands, giving it a gentle squeeze at first. The pressure becomes harder and deeper as he continues to work me over.

As my body becomes increasingly aroused, I find myself parting my legs even more so that now each leg is resting on the edges of the table. Every time Jack's hands wind up on my bottom, I find myself rocking my hips upwards, inviting him to massage my inner thighs and that tender spot between my legs which is now dripping with excitement. He only grazes these parts of me—such a tease.

Since he is still standing at the head of the table, I move my hands so that they come in contact with his legs. As they travel upwards towards his waist he moves his hands towards my ass. When I squeeze his firm cheeks, he does the same to me. When my hand moves to the front of his pants, he slowly slides two fingers down the center of my back and lightly caresses my bottom with the tip of one finger. He slips another under my thong until the very tip of his middle finger is slick with my excitement.

I gasp when his finger enters me and can't remember the last time I was that excited. While I am rocking my hips upward to give him more of an angle for deeper entry, he removes his finger from inside me and I feel empty inside.

"Turn around."

Gasping for air, I do as I am told and am now on my back. Jack reaches for the pillow that is kept under the table and places it under my neck; my eyes are closed and my mouth agape. He bends down to kiss my forehead and then runs his tongue down my nose and rests his mouth on my lips. In this sexual game of chicken, I lose and my lips part first.

When Jack's tongue enters my mouth, my body shakes with the feeling of electricity. Without realizing what I am doing, I move my right hand down my stomach and start touching myself. Jack sees this and moves the offending hand aside.

"That is mine, not yours." He takes my hands and places them over my head. "I still need to stretch you."

Jack goes over to his workout bag and removes something from it —a blindfold. After placing it over my eyes, he walks around to the end of the table where my feet are and quietly slides his own shorts off. He parts my legs and kneels before me on the table, resting my calves on his shoulders, and slowly pushes my legs towards the head of the table where he keeps them pinned by my ears. My ass is tight from our workout, so this is painful, but pain slowly gives way to pleasure.

He runs his arousal up and down my thong, starting at the top where his head pushes onto my pearl and ending down at the bottom of my opening, which is by now dripping and swelling with excitement—and anticipation.

"What do you want, Libby?" he whispers into my ear

"I want you inside me." My legs go weak; I am full of passion and throw all caution to the wind.

Jack rests my legs back on the table; I lift my hips and slide my fingers under the waist of my thong to remove it, but Jack intercepts me.

"These are now mine," he says while he rips them off, causing me to gasp once again.

Rubbing his head up and down my lips, he enters me slowly, teasing me with just the tip at first and then gradually slides deeper until his rock-hard entirety is deep inside me. He grabs my right hand from over my head and places it on top of my mound.

"Rub it."

I don't hesitate, and massage myself until I climax with a shudder; it's the most intense orgasm I've ever had. It is clear that Jack hasn't climaxed yet as he is still rock hard inside me—The Rock of Westport indeed.

Jack surprises me by sliding out.

"Stand up." This is what has been missing from my life over the past few years, a man who knows what he wants and isn't afraid to

ask for it…and take it!

I stand up but keep the blindfold on.

"Bend over the table."

I am obedient.

Jack bends down to kiss between my parted cheeks and then returns to push himself between my lips, slowly rocking in and out— as he does so, I feel my passion building again. I've heard about women who've had multiple orgasms but never experienced one myself. The myth is about to become reality after Jack enters me as deep as he can and moves his hands from my hips over to the front of my body where he uses the pointer fingers on each of his hands to massage my pearl.

As I climax for the second time, Jack releases into me. With every pulse of his excitement, I moan in pleasure having what feels like mini convulsions while Jack's seed rushes inside.

I turn around, remove the blindfold, and lay my eyes on Jack Gregory's naked body for the first time that day. The sight of his strong shoulders, chiseled chest, and contoured stomach makes my pulse race once again. I look down and see that, amazingly, he is still rock hard. This was no time to think of my husband, but Terry always needs a good twenty-minute reset time before starting up again —by the looks of things, Jack is ready to go.

I wrap my arms around his neck and pull him closer. Once our lips meet, I pull Jack inside me, and we do it again.

#

Having been in the tub for a solid twenty minutes that morning, I knew it was time to get on with my day. I pulled the plug and sat in the water as it receded below my shoulders. Once it was empty, I got out, toweled off, and then walked naked through my room to my giant walk-in closet where I was about to make the hardest decision I had to make that day—what to wear for afternoon drinks with Marley.

CHAPTER SIX

Playing A Round

As I think back on that fantasy, it still makes me shudder. To keep this story going, though, you need to know what happened at the golf course that morning and for that I'm going to share Terry's recollection of his match.

I'll be honest, though, I decided to edit some things out of this part of Terry's story—I kept the sex stuff in his earlier chapter because it is integral to our story, but he decided to go into a lot of detail about his golf match with Preston and my instinct tells me that most people don't really care that they were all square going into the eighteenth but that Preston parred the final hole while my husband took bogey.

I will share with you the *highlights* of his match, though, because what happened at the course that Sunday lit the fuse that led directly to the dynamite that had been building up inside me for some time. Note, whatever you see in italics on the coming pages are some comments I have for Terry—I've learned that humor is a great healer and inflect some snarky comments into his reflections from time to time to aid with my own healing process.

\#

That morning I pulled into the club's driveway and got a parking spot close to the building that housed all of the members' golf clubs. On my walk to the building, I was intercepted by Cassidy Clarke, one of the senior partners of my firm. *This woman has a turkey neck.* It looked as if she had just finished playing and was returning her clubs.

"Big round for you, Terry. Don't expect Preston to go easy on you and don't you dare let him win."

I had my pick of law firms after graduating number one in my class at New York Law School, but what pushed Hewson, Evans, Clayton & Mullen over the edge was the free membership to Westport's exclusive Nyala Farms Country Club—all employees had one, even the junior associates. *I wished they didn't.*

The game of golf was so ingrained in my firm's culture that management rated employees by using the golf terms under par (high performer), par (average performer), and over par (under performer) during our annual review process. *Golf is so confusing, under par sounds worse than over par. Idiots.* Further, if an employee was told that they made an eagle for a client, that was high praise, whereas double bogey meant someone was going to have a talking to with firm management and possibly face disciplinary action.

"I think I'll hold my own out there," I said confidently —the firm had no room for humility. *Why was he so humble in our bedroom?*

"Word of advice, Terry, don't think, know." *Gobble gobble, you pretentious bitch.*

That was the same phrase my high school English teacher would use—it bugged me in high school and it still bugged me last year when Cassidy muttered it—not that I would admit as much to a senior partner.

"Thank you, Cassidy. I'll keep that in mind."

With that, Cassidy Clarke walked back towards the clubhouse and I approached a staff member to get my bag.

"Bag 269 please, Tyler."

"Walking or riding today, Mr. Gardner?" the young man asked.

"Walking," I replied. Carts were never used when firm employees played with each other—they were viewed as a sign of weakness and the firm made it very clear there was no room for weak employees. *Only fragile egos.*

I slung the bag over my shoulder and walked towards the clubhouse where Preston was expecting me for coffee.

I had been at the firm for fourteen years; this July—just two short months away—would mark my fifteenth anniversary. While I was given the opportunity to defer my start date to September and spend a few months after graduation doing, well, whatever I wanted, I was eager to get started so turned that opportunity down. *Who turns down the opportunity to do whatever they want for two months while a guaranteed job waited for them? Idiot.*

"Eagle" associates who routinely performed under par typically made partner anywhere between fifteen years and eighteen years in. This was longer than most other firms, but mine was very selective with who made partner because once admitted into that exclusive club, your ticket was punched and all material worries would drift away.

Importantly, it wasn't just our performance at work that provided the path to partnership—young up-and-comers had to say all the right things at social and networking functions and approach every challenge with the ruthlessness and vigor that the firm's reputation was built on. I knew that how I played this round might be the nail in the coffin of my time as an associate, because if I won, I'd be that much closer to being named partner. Little did I know, it would lead to the nail in the coffin of my marriage. *No comment.*

I walked into the clubhouse and found Preston sitting at a table reading the newspaper. The front page had a story about a group of lawmakers looking to make marijuana legal in Connecticut and when Preston saw me, he wasted no time expressing his opinions on the matter.

"I know that you have an interest in this topic, Terry, but I'll let you know right now, I'm not a fan."

As if I didn't know—Preston was one of these uptight guys who could drink half a handle of Dewar's a day, but something like weed was out of the question. Ironically, if there's anyone who could benefit from a toke or two, it was Pres.

"My interest isn't based on my personal appreciation for cannabis, I don't touch the stuff, but Connecticut has a budget crisis and our governor is constantly spending money we don't have. People are going to smoke pot anyway, we may as well get some tax revenue for it. Right now, we are leaving a lot of money on the table." *He and I used to get high as kites and make love. I wonder if he remembers that.*

"I understand economics, I just worry about the message it sends to young people."

This guy must live under a rock if he thinks young people can't easily get their hands on weed when they want to—weed that's usually tainted with all sorts of other crap. If the government regulated it, at least the stuff sold over the counter would be pure. I expressed as much to Preston and then added my thoughts on how legalization would reduce drug-related crimes.

"The minute we legalize marijuana, the Mexican cartels will stop producing and importing it—they know how to cut their losses. It's better than building a wall." *I love it when he talks dirty.*

"That's where we disagree." Preston raised his voice. "Yes, they will quit production of pot, but cartels aren't stupid. They will take the efforts they'd placed against cultivating cannabis and simply transfer them to production of harder stuff—cocaine, heroin, meth. Make no mistake, they are market makers."

I hate it when he's right, but I knew that conceding the point would be like conceding a stroke in the match we were about to play. I played back what I learned in Colorado, figuring he was the guy who approved the request to attend the conference and that recalling what I learned might remind him that I had his approval to go.

"Colorado's budget crisis is a memory. Schools are fully funded for the first time in decades, the state's transportation infrastructure is top notch, and drug-related crime is down."

"And sales of junk food are going through the roof." It was a rare moment of humor from the typically stoic Preston.

"The last thing I'll say about the matter is to proceed in this field with caution and I'll remind you that if I ever learn that you are using this stuff recreationally it will be the end of your career at the firm. To our clients, our interest in cannabis must be purely for business reasons—

we have a zero-tolerance policy for illicit drug use at Hewson, Evans, Clayton & Mullen. *Fucking squares.*

After that conversation we went back outside, grabbed our bags, and I played as if I was in a sudden death match to win one of golf's majors—though I lost the match on the very last hole when I conceded a five-inch putt to Preston.

"That's good," I said before he went to putt it in.

Having lost my match on the last hole, I removed my cap, shook Preston's hand, and went back to the clubhouse to shower. We regrouped at the bar and once I sat down he wasted no time getting down to business.

"Hell of a match, Terry. You showed a lot of skill out there and a willingness to take risks. That shot over the trees to cut the corner on seven was ballsy."

"Thank you. Your going for it on eighteen was admirable—if I were a betting man, I would have put money on your laying up."

"You underestimated me," Preston said with a laugh. "And it looks as if I may have overestimated you."

He must have seen the blood rush from my face as he didn't waste any time expanding on his thoughts.

"Excuse me," I interrupted, "but…"

"Hear me out. Now you've got three senior partners thinking you are the next coming of Christ and three who feel as if you are just not ready."

My firm has six senior partners who run the place and make all decisions on which associates become partners. As of today, I knew I had three in my corner and two who were firm nos—Preston was the holdout. If I impressed him, then his nod of approval would have given me the majority I needed to clear the hurdle, but apparently I didn't do what I needed to get him on my side.

"How did you overestimate me?"

"On eighteen you gave me a gimme on my last putt."

"There was no way you would miss it, I was simply being polite. You did the same for me on sixteen." My ball was within three inches of the cup and Preston gave me the putt. In match play, it is very common to give your opponent a gimme when the putt is within a few inches of the hole.

He looked at me in the eyes and said, "Never concede the putt that beats you. You have to fight until the bitter end. What would our clients think if you conceded a pivotal point in a case?"

I took a sip on the drink that the bartender had left in front of me after I first sat down.

"But we have a problem, Terry. You see, for the first time in a while, the senior partners are absolutely deadlocked on promoting a senior associate to partner, and that means we need to send you down to Florida to meet with Paul."

The Paul who Preston was speaking of was Paul Hewson, the founding partner of our firm. Evans, Clayton, and Mullen were all fictional names to make the firm sound bigger than it was when Paul started it—there was no doubt about it, Paul Hewson was the head honcho —he was our god and thought of himself as such.

"I'm sending you down to Fort Lauderdale for three days to shadow with Paul. You'll spend Tuesday through Thursday with him. He's your tiebreaker."

I had just been thrown a lifeline, but there was a big problem—Libby was having an art exhibition Thursday night and I promised her I'd be there. She'd been planning it for months and made it very clear that my not going was not an option. Just as I was about to ask if I could meet with him another week, Preston beat me to it.

"He's leaving for Ireland on Friday to spend a few weeks back home. You'll only get one chance to have so much time with Paul, so don't even think about asking whether or not there's another week you could do. Word of advice though," Preston said.

"What's that?" I asked.

"Paul is a little, how do I put this, different. Keep an open mind around him—he's a bit unpredictable."

According to the rumors the other associates heard about the man, that was putting it mildly. None of us had ever met him or even seen him in person and there were all sorts of rumors floating around about our eccentric founder.

"I'll keep that in mind,"

That was settled then—I knew what I had to do in order to make partner and I wasn't going to blow that opportunity. *I still resent him for this.* All I had to do was figure out how I was going to break the news to Libby. *That was a conversation I'd rather forget.*

CHAPTER SEVEN

Marley's Tell

While Terry was finishing his round with Preston, Marley and I met at the Duck for drinks. I felt like a new woman after my bath and she picked up on how relaxed I seemed.

"What's up with you, chica? You are practically glowing."

I blushed, took a sip of my drink, and waved my right hand at her and wiggled my middle finger. Marley and I keep no secrets from each other.

"Ohhh, someone had a date with themselves I see," she replied. "You should remind yourself what the real thing feels like sometime."

Just when I thought she was going to lecture me on cutting Terry off, and subsequently denying myself penetrative sex, her phone buzzed on the table and took away her attention. Saved by a buzz twice in one day!

"Shit!" Marley exclaimed after looking at her phone.

"What?" I asked.

"Claire can't go to Chicago tomorrow and she asked if I could go in her place."

Marley is a marketing consultant, a focus group moderator, to be more specific. She travels around the country running market research studies, testing out new product concepts, advertising ideas, and uncovers insights into consumers that her clients then use against us to get us to buy more stuff. It's a pretty cool job that allows her to keep a pretty open schedule when she's not traveling.

"What happened?"

"Her kid is sick and needs to stay home."

"Why can't her husband take care of the kid so she can do her job?" I asked.

"He's like your hubby—his job comes first, everything else takes a back seat."

"How long will you be there until? Please don't tell me you are going to miss my exhibition."

"Just overnight," she replied and took a sip of her drink. "I'll be there, chica, don't worry your pretty little head about it."

"Good," I replied. "Because I need you and Terry there. It's a big night for me—there's a who's who of Westport society coming."

"When did you go from being the bohemian chick I knew and loved to being at the epicenter of Westport socialites anyway?"

It was true, over time I had shed my bohemian ways and embraced the lifestyle that my husband was able to afford for us. At the time, though, I rationalized that I had an *if you can't beat 'em join 'em mentality*, but I now realized that I changed every bit as Terry did—I just didn't want to admit it.

"She's still in here," I said, pointing to my heart. "Hey, we are here and not at some chichi place drinking twenty-dollar Cosmos, aren't we?"

"Who the fuck do you think you are talking to, Libby Gardner?" Marley said while rolling her eyes. "I know exactly why we're here," she said and then turned around and nodded towards the eye candy behind the bar.

Nate, the Duck's Sunday mixologist, stood at six two and had long dark hair that just covered his chestnut-colored eyes. His arms gave away the fact he spent a lot of time in the gym and his face was like that of an angel— not that I'd been paying any attention to angels recently— I don't think they bother showing up on my shoulder anymore.

"I see the way you look at him, chica, and how you conveniently chose the seat facing the bar."

"So what, he's cute."

"And you are married!"

"It's so hard to call it a marriage anymore. All he does is work and he doesn't even give me the time of day."

"Who cut who off in the bedroom?"

Not this again, I thought to myself. "If he were more attentive, I'd let him knock on heaven's door."

"Girl, you just got to tell him what you want. Give it to him straight…and then give it to him good," she laughed.

"I need a refill," I said and then moved to get up and head towards the bar.

"Nope," Marley said and sprang out of her chair. "This one's on me."

I watched her go up to the bar and felt a twinge of jealousy at all the attention she received from guys. I still had my looks, but Marley's pale skin and long red hair were so alluring that guys—and girls for that matter— couldn't help but stare. I still got some looks, but she could do something about it whereas I couldn't.

I could easily see that she was flirting with Nate. It almost killed me when she looked over in my direction and winked while biting her lip right after ordering. I then saw her reach over the bar and write something on Nate's hand before returning with our cocktails.

"What was that all about?" I asked, unable to hide the edge in my tone of voice.

"He told me he just broke up with his girlfriend, so I gave him my number," Marley said and then pursed her lips around her straw and took a sip of her drink.

"Life isn't fair," I said, and then did the same.

"You know I love you, right, chica?"

"Of course," I said reluctantly and anticipated that her chosen setup was going to lead to some tough love. I wasn't disappointed.

"You have to have a sit-down with that man and tell him what is going on in your head. You've been together for almost twenty years and married for fifteen. You at least owe that to him."

I knew that what she was saying was the truth but didn't want to hear it.

"Here is what I suggest you do, Libby."

"This should be good," I said and rolled my eyes.

"After we leave here, I want you to go home and put on the sluttiest piece of lingerie you have."

"I thought you said this was about talking with him."

"Who says you can't have a little fun while you chat? Believe me, this will get his attention. So get into something sexy and then lure him into the bedroom and get him to lie on his back."

"What, and let him fuck me?"

"No! You tell him that you two need to have a little chat. Straddle his lap and rock your hips back and forth to get him excited. When you feel his arousal, bend over and whisper into his ear that he works too hard and that you need him home more."

"A man with a hard-on will promise anything," I argued.

"This isn't just any man with a hard-on, this is your man with a hard-on."

She took a moment to look me square in the eyes.

"Continue."

"Then, as you feel his erection pushing up on you, stop."

"Stop?"

"Yes, stop. It will drive him nuts. Walk out of the room and don't come back. On your way out, peel off a trail of the clothes you are wearing and go into another room."

"Why do I get the feeling that you have done something like this before?"

"I have. Works every time when I need to have a conversation with a guy."

"And what happens when he finds me?"

"Tell him everything that's on your mind and express your concern over the distance that has come between you."

"While I'm naked in the guest bedroom?"

"Consider it a way of baring your soul to him."

"And then what."

"Tell him to take his clothes off but that he can't touch you until he tells you how he feels."

"And what if that leads to an argument?" I asked.

Marley countered with, "What if it leads to great sex?"

"What if I don't want great sex and I want an argument?"

Marley countered with, "It's scientifically proven that two people who are in the same room together naked cannot get into an argument." Marley broke eye contact and sipped her drink and offered a devilish smile.

"You are just fucking with me, aren't you?"

Marley gave me a mischievous look and giggled.

"Yeah, that was going nowhere," she admitted and then added, "but I do think you should stop the moratorium on intercourse you've got that man under. It's only going to hurt both of you in the end."

"I didn't come here to be interrogated," I stated. This wasn't turning out to be the relaxing afternoon I'd planned. It's a good thing I Ubered to the bar, because there was definitely a third drink in my future.

"Just tell me this and I'll drop it," Marley said. "What's the biggest complaint you have about Terry, his big income? His giant cock?" Apparently, her memory of that art class was as vivid as mine.

I didn't have to think about it at all. "All he cares about is work. He doesn't put me first anymore."

"But it's his work that affords you the lifestyle you have. Could it be that he actually is putting you first but that you just don't recognize it?"

"Jesus Christ, Marley, I never wanted to be married to a fucking lawyer." My tone gave away the fact that I wanted this discussion to be over. Marley, the Dominant that she was, wasn't deterred by my verbal lashing.

"How would you feel if you saw him in bed with someone else?" she asked.

I looked at her and replied, "He already has a mistress,

his law firm."

"Libby, I'm telling you right now you are playing with fire. Your husband is hot, has a killer job, and has a lot to offer. He's a catch, chica, everyone can see it but you."

"If I didn't know any better, Marley, I'd think that you want to fuck him."

She averted her eyes and focused them on her drink; a tell if I'd ever seen one. So that was it, she had a thing for Terry.

"I don't want to see you hurt, chica."

"I'll be fine," I said and then headed towards Nate the Great to get two more drinks.

#

I now know that Marley was right—I should have been more open with Terry about how I was feeling and with what I wanted from him physically. Why is it that we expect our partners to know what we want through some kind of osmosis? I'm now aware that we have to break down the barriers that make it so hard for men and women to have honest conversations about sex in order to have truly fulfilling relationships. Of course, this is the wiser Libby Gardner talking—I've changed so much over the past year. Thank you, PET!

CHAPTER EIGHT

Dropping the Bomb

While the one year older and wiser Libby Gardner now has a tool box of interpersonal resources including I-Feel statements and active listening skills, I want to be crystal clear on one thing—I would not change a thing about how I reacted when Terry broke the news that he decided to take a last-minute business trip the week of my art exhibition.

It's important for you to know that, at the moment Terry came home, a hangover was setting in—that's what sucks about day drinking, it feels fun at the time but instead of sleeping it off, you get a stinger at the same time most people start prepping dinner, and this wasn't good news for Terry.

I could tell when he walked in that something was bothering him because he had a hard time making eye contact and decided to go right to the sink and clean the dishes instead of talk to me. He was passive like that and historically would procrastinate for a while before addressing whatever issue he needed to address. I wasn't in the mood for the guessing game and had no patience for waiting, so I spoke up and beat him to it.

"What's the matter?"

He looked at his shoes.

"Did something happen on the course today?"

He started cleaning a dish he'd already cleaned.

"What the fuck is the matter, Terry?" I didn't have it in me that night—between my growing hangover and the emotional roller coaster Marley had me on during the afternoon, I just wanted him to grow a pair and tell me what he needed to tell me.

"I lost my match with Preston," he finally said.

This is what golf and law do to people, change their perspectives so that the smallest events become big deals. It was just a match, there's always a winner and a loser, so why the hell was he so down about it?

"Okay, so, why are you in such a funk?"

"It's not that I lost the match. I played well! You should have seen my shot on…"

I cut him off—I couldn't give a rat's ass about his shot on whatever hole he was about to reminisce on. The man hadn't noticed me for weeks, but I bet he could give me a vivid description of the azaleas at Augusta National.

"The point?" I pressed him.

"Preston said the senior partners are split on whether or not I should be promoted to partner. I have to participate in a tie-breaker."

My patience level was razor thin. Perhaps if I were a better wife, I'd have approached him, given him a hug, and rubbed his back. Maybe, if I were the ideal woman from the 1950s, I would have asked him if he wanted to talk about it and be the listener he needed me to be and then welcome him into my bed and make him feel loved. Instead I said this, "That place is going to be the death of me."

Terry gave me a blank stare and then some switch inside him flicked and he raised his voice.

"The death of you? It's my career on the line, Libby, not to mention our future. But I'm glad to know you care."

He stormed out of the kitchen. Instead of following him, I stayed where I was at the kitchen table.

"I don't want to get into the work argument tonight, Terry, I'm not in the mood," I shouted down the hall.

"You are never in the mood for anything," he said from the living room.

And there it was, the passive aggressive sex comment. Why not kill two birds with one stone and tackle the sex argument along with the career argument at the same time?

"What's that supposed to mean?" I asked, even though I knew exactly what he meant.

His head popped back into the kitchen and he looked me directly in the eyes.

"We haven't had sex in 99 days."

That sounded about right, but I wasn't going to give him the satisfaction of acknowledging our dry spell. "I didn't know you were counting."

He just gave me a look that suggested he didn't want to talk about it anymore—that made two of us. I didn't push it because my head was pounding. Why did I have that fourth drink? Oh, maybe it was because I'd figured out that my best friend wanted to bone my husband.

"This isn't about sex, Terry, or golf. Just tell me what's

the matter."

He looked away and let out a deep breath. "I have to leave for Florida tomorrow night. I have meetings Tuesday through Thursday with the firm's founder, Paul Hewson. He's the tie-breaker on whether or not they make me a partner."

So that was it, this was his way of telling me that he wasn't coming to my art show, instead he was going to spend time with an aging eccentric lawyer who, I imagined, looked like a cross between Jeff Goldblum and a fruit fly.

"No!" I blurted out. "You are not doing this to me."

"Look, I am going to fly out tomorrow night and I'll take the earliest possible flight back on Thursday. I'll make it to your show."

He tried his hardest to sound sincere, but deep down inside I knew he didn't believe what he'd just said.

Terry had every right to be nervous—I'd been planning this exhibition of my work for months; as much as I eschewed my neighbors and their one-percenter ways, I was putting on this event for a good cause, and their money was going to help me make it a success. I was raising money for a charity started by a famous actor who called Westport home before his death—his foundation raises money to give kids with cancer opportunities they otherwise wouldn't have. Like other business owners in Westport, I wanted to do my part in helping the foundation and it was important for me to have my husband's support that Thursday night. The combination of my hangover and extreme disappointment led to an eruption that hadn't been seen in the United States since Mount St. Helens blew in 1980.

I started by throwing a plate at him, which missed by a few inches. My aim with the glass was much better; fortunately, he hadn't been drinking and his reflexes were sharp and he swatted it away with his hand.

With nothing left within reach to throw at him, I simply charged at him and started slapping him while tears came down my face.

"How could you fucking do this to me?"

I kept hitting him and then he did something he hadn't done in a long time, he wrapped his arms around me and whispered, "Libby, I'm sorry."

Make no mistake, those words meant nothing to me at the time, but now I know he was sincere. He was truly sorry and conflicted about breaking a promise to me, but his work eventually won out and he made the wrong call. I didn't let him off the hook and broke through his grasp.

"I'm going to lie down. Don't follow me and don't plan on sleeping in our room tonight."

I didn't wait for a response. I just stormed down the hall, slammed the door, and climbed into bed.

Terry slept on the couch—and that was the last time I'd actually see him before things when to shit on Thursday night. I was still asleep the next morning when he got ready for work and he left for Florida from his office.

The only thing I had going for me was the fact that I had a training session with Jack the next morning—if Terry's news about his having to miss my exhibition was the match, my training session with Jack was the fuse. My art exhibition, as you will see, was the dynamite.

CHAPTER NINE

Pop

Terry's experiences in Florida are key to fully understanding The Event, though to get the full effect of what happened there, you really have to hear it from him because I wasn't there. I'll say this, I have to hand it to him—just as I have come a long way in the past twelve months, so has he.

#

Here's how I knew my life was all about to go south once I'd arrived in Florida, my father met me at the airport. I have to give it to Libby, the woman knew how to get me, and calling my dad to let him know I was coming to Florida was a masterful move in her quest to make my time down there miserable. *He deserved it.*

I remember feeling my phone vibrate while descending the escalator and checked it to find it was a text from Libby's friend Marley asking me to call her as soon as I could. I've known her as long as I've known Libby and consider her one of my best friends, so it's not unusual for her to text me, and lately she'd been reaching out to see how I was doing knowing that Libby and I were going through a rough patch.

I replied that I'd call her once I got settled in my hotel and then looked up from my phone to see Pop waiting for me at the bottom of the escalator, standing out like a sore thumb in-between all of the livery drivers dressed in their dark suits. They all carried placards with last names like Allen, Ahlers, and O'Connell on them—my father's sign read Hemingway.

Pop is a joyous fellow—much like Dickens' Ghost of Christmas Present, though he was never accompanied by a feast or wearing long, flowing velour robes. Tie-dye was more his bag, along with a scent that carried with it the suggestion that Woodstock, for him, lasted more than three days—it lasted his entire adulthood.

We were close once, right up until the time I decided to quit a career in writing and publishing to attend law school. To my siblings he would refer to me as "sell-out." It stung at the time, but I get it now. *He was right.*

I was raised to have a strong contempt for anything institutional. The Man was out to get us, or so my father preached. He blamed his lack of achievement on everything other than himself. The fact he couldn't hold down a steady job had nothing to do with him. Of course it was his boss who just didn't understand Pop's way of doing things. My mom leaving him? It wasn't the fact that he freely gave himself to whoever would share his bed— she just didn't get that he was a lion who couldn't be tamed.

I broke his heart when I told him I was going into law, and things have never been the same since. However, when I spotted him in his purple and orange Grateful

Dead tee as I rode the escalator down to baggage claim at Fort Lauderdale International Airport, he was all smiles— I assumed he was high.

As I got closer I noticed that his hair had receded pretty far back and the gray wiry locks he had left were pulled into a tight ponytail that was tucked under his tee-shirt. He looked different, and I realized I hadn't seen him in five years. He must have lost a good twenty pounds.

I was raised in South Florida; the first time I left was to move into college back in the mid 1990s. I've only been back a handful of times since, most recently five years ago when Libby and I spent Christmas with Pop and my siblings and helped him move out of my childhood home.

"Welcome home, Hemingway," he said when I was close enough to hear. He called me that because when I was a teenager I never went anywhere without a journal. I used to write in these black marble composition books and he took to calling me the name of his favorite writer with the hopes that, one day, I'd publish my own Great American Novel.

"Dressed to impress as always, Pop." He was never Father or Dad, he was always Pop. "Libby tell you I was coming down?"

"She sure did. Now why is it I have to hear from my daughter-in-law that my son is coming to Florida?"

He tried to hug me, but I extended my hand instead. *Asshole move.*

"Maybe because you refer to me as a sell-out and have taken zero interest in my career ever since I decided to become a lawyer."

"I just called you Hemingway."

"I haven't written in years, Pop."

"Well that's a shame, you were so good at it. Your bags are coming in on carousel five."

When I walked past the baggage carousel he mentioned, he repeated himself to make sure I heard him.

"I need to go to where they have the oversized bags."

"What did you bring, a body?"

"No, my golf clubs."

"That's worse."

Pop hates golf, just another thing that he and Libby have in common. *Another reason why I loved him.*

I had to wait a few minutes for my clubs to come out and once they did we were off to the parking garage. Once my sticks were in his trunk, I told him to take me to the Hilton on Fort Lauderdale Beach, which was the hotel my firm always puts me up at.

"Change of plans," he said.

All I could think to myself was, oh no she didn't. *Oh yes I did.*

"You are staying with me at Yasgur's."

If you needed any more proof that life isn't fair, my father—who always skated through life fueled by a diet of reckless abandon and illicit substances—won the lottery. I don't mean that in the metaphorical sense, the man won fifty million dollars playing Powerball.

Playing against type, he took a portion of that money and set it aside as savings. With the remainder, he bought an old roadside beach motel between Fort Lauderdale and Pompano and re-named it Yasgur's Farm South as a reference to the farm in upstate New York where the first Woodstock Festival was held. It's a place aging hippies can go to live out their golden years; I couldn't think of anything more hellish.

"Pop, I really don't…"

He cut me off before I could finish my protest. "I'm sure you don't, but it is what it is, now there's just one stop we have to make before going home."

This should be good.

"Where are we going?"

"I've got to see a man about some produce."

Jesus Christ, he was going to take me to score some weed. The man was now a multimillionaire but still ventured out to score his own herb.

"Don't they deliver now?"

"I like the thrill of scoring on the street, reminds me of the old days."

"Do you even remember the old days?"

He looks at me with a laugh, "I remember when you weren't a square."

I know that I've changed since I was an idealistic teenager, but that's all part of maturing, right? Someone had to be the adult in the parent-child relationship; it clearly wasn't going to be Pop, so it had to be me.

He drove us north on A1A—the road that parallels the beach—and even though it was the late evening there were still people walking alongside the water.

"The season's just about over," he remarked. "Pretty soon all the snowbirds will head back north and it will be nice and quiet again. Pains in the ass."

He then went on to say something about the cops being extra hard on South Florida's aging hippie population, arguing that well-to-do snowbirds complained about their unsightly appearance and that their presence drags property values down. The mayor, who knew how important tourism dollars are to the city's economy, had encouraged the city's finest to harass the hippies and my father had been the target of numerous stop-and-frisk searchers.

"That's why I never carry outside of Yasgur's. Even though possession is a small misdemeanor down here, I don't need that hassle."

"Maybe if you cut the ponytail and tried to fit in more, they wouldn't bother you so much."

This clearly upset Pop. "You may have sold your soul to The Man, Terry, but mine is pure. This hair ain't goin' nowhere, and if you think I'm going to start walking around wearing polo shirts with a little whale on it, you must be smoking something funny. Which reminds me, we are just about there."

We parked in front of an old beach-side stand adjacent to the Pompano Beach fishing pier. When I was a kid, my grandparents lived in a condo in walking distance to it and I spent just about every weekend here with my three siblings. As we got out and walked towards the pier, I could almost see myself as a kid on the beach running towards the water.

"You, Greg, Mia, and Jimmy used to have a lot of fun on this beach," he said, mentioning my siblings. I hadn't seen them in years either—part of me felt bad about that, but keeping in touch was a two-way street and my phone wasn't exactly ringing off the hook at the time.

"We sure did, Pop."

We walked towards a public bathroom that was housed in the pier. I felt a twinge of sadness when I saw that the Fisherman's Wharf restaurant that we enjoyed many meals at when I was growing up was closed. It represented a happier time in my life—a time when I lived more in the moment and had fewer cares. The weekends we spent here left happy memories and being back tugged at my heartstrings.

"Remember the conch chowder?" my father asked as we passed the boarded-up restaurant."

"Spicy as hell," I said.

As I walked on the stand and thought of my past, my mind imagined that I was walking in my old footprints preserved in the sand from the days of my childhood. I didn't think about that time in my life often, why was I thinking of it now?

I felt something stir in me and thought maybe I had been too hard on Pop and maybe I should have been more proactive in getting in touch with my siblings, but just as I was about to admit as much to my father, we got intercepted by Wilfred—a tall and thin Jamaican man with a wide smile, dreadlocks that fell down to his waist, and a cloud of smoke around him that shouted what his profession was.

"Hey Gerry, who dat white boy wit ya?"

"Wilfred, I'd like you to meet my boy, Terry."

"Awe dis you boy? Let me takea look atcha. Yes, mon, ju have his eyes. You lucky to have a man like Gerry as a fadda."

Yes, lucky. My father, who's about to take me home to his hippie commune on the beach, had driven me from the airport to score some pot—it just doesn't get any better than this. *He became such a fucking square.*

"Come to my office, mon," Wilfred said to my father and they walked inside the men's room.

"Come with me, Terry," Pop said. "It will look funny if you are waiting outside a men's room by yourself."

Right, but going into a men's room after hours with a Rastafarian and an aging hippie would look totally legit. Against my better judgment, I followed them in.

"How much you need, mon?"

"Two ounces should do."

Two ounces? Was he buying for the whole commune?

"You know da price, mon."

My father reached into his pocket, counted off some bills, and handed a wad of cash to Wilfred, who in turn gave him two ziplock bags of grass. The stamp on it said Mindfuck—there was no mistaking what effect this strain was meant to have.

My father opened a bag and put it to his nose, and that's when it all went to shit. The door to the men's room burst open and two officers from the Pompano Beach police department's vice unit stormed in.

"Police, hands up," they shouted in unison.

My father, with the weed still in his hands, raised his hands above his head. I did the same as a cop swung me around for a frisking that violated me so much I was surprised I hadn't been asked to cough.

"He's clear."

No hernia either.

Wilfred and Pop were also frisked; Pop was relieved of his recent purchase and Wilfred was relieved of everything he had on him, which, unfortunately for him, included more than just marijuana.

"Come on, mon, it's just a little herb and some painkillas," Wilfred protested.

"We've warned you about selling here, Wilfred," one of the cops said.

"Hey, mon, I'm just helping my friend Gerry wit his

glaucoma."

"By the looks of it," one of the cops said, "there's enough here to treat a retirement home full of glaucoma patients."

One cop cuffed Wilfred and then led him out of the bathroom.

"Can we leave now?" I asked the officer who remained behind.

"You in a hurry?" one of them said to me. "I'm going to need to see your identification."

"Why?" I questioned.

"Because I'm the fucking cop, I have the fucking badge, and I'm going to give you both a fucking ticket."

My father reached into his pocket and handed over his license. I didn't.

"Come on, junior, I haven't got all day."

"What are you giving me a ticket for?" I asked. I was angry as I hadn't done anything wrong.

"If you don't shut up, it will be for possession with intent to sell."

"I wasn't in possession of anything."

"Terry," my father spoke up, "just hand him your license."

"Listen to the old man, Terry."

"I'm a lawyer, and what you are doing isn't right."

When my father heard me say this, he shut his eyes and said, "Oh no."

I quickly learned that there is nothing cops hate more than being told they can't do something—especially from lawyers.

"Have it your way." He reached for his handcuffs.

"Okay, okay," I said and then reached into my pocket,

removed my wallet, fished my license out, and handed it over to the officer who wrote out two tickets.

"Westport. Didn't Paul Newman live here?"

"Yep," I said. "You a fan?"

"Of his acting, no. Of his racing, yes."

The officer finished writing the tickets and handed them to us along with our licenses.

"Don't even think about protesting them. Oh, and congratulations, your names will be in the paper this week."

Just when I thought things couldn't get any worse.

"We weren't arrested, why are they going to be in the paper?"

"Anyone who gets a citation for possession automatically gets their name in the police blotter. While we can't arrest you anymore, the mayor feels as if public shame is a strong deterrent."

After the officer left, we walked back to Pop's car and he could tell I was fuming.

"I don't know why you are so upset, I just spent two hundred bucks on weed that Officer Skunknuts back there is most likely going to smoke or sell himself."

"I can't have my name in the paper, pop."

"Relax, who the hell do you know reads the *Pompano Beach Gazette*?"

Most likely all the wrong people.

CHAPTER TEN

An Invitation

There's much more to Terry's time in Florida, but I'm going to take a break from sharing that part of the story with you because it's important to know what I did the day Terry left.

I woke up to find that Terry had already gone to work and knew that I wouldn't be seeing him until he got back from his trip—which was very likely going to be after my art show. While I was bummed about that, I did have something to look forward to—my Monday morning training session with Jack Gregory. Since we did legs on Friday, I knew today he'd focus on chest, shoulders, and triceps, which meant I'd spend a lot of time on my back looking up at him.

I decided to wear the shortest pair of shorts I had for the session, along with a top that was definitely a little too tight around my chest. In my past near misses I had never been the aggressor, but with Terry down in Florida and his recent decision to put his job over my art show, I became more brazen with my urge to stray.

Since it was a warm spring day, Jack came to the house dressed to work out wearing a form-fitting shirt that showed off his muscles—Jesus Christ, even his muscles had muscles. During the winter months, he'd wear warm-up pants, but given the turn in the weather, he had on a pair of shorts that showed off his legs. The man had quads like tree trunks and the most defined calves I'd ever seen.

As I laid my eyes upon him for the first time that day, I felt a tingle inside the center of my belly, a tingle that would travel its way downward as my mind wandered during our workout.

After a quick warmup on the treadmill, we went to my bench and did some dumbbell presses. I was on my back looking up towards him and almost lost concentration as I caught a glimpse of what was under his shorts. I normally don't get excited by a man's package, but as my eyes drifted up Jack's leg, I felt a pang of anticipation build in me. It was covered by his tight briefs, but there was no mistaking what was underneath, and my pulse was racing. What was happening?

As we switched from chest to shoulders, Jack came up from behind to spot me on shoulder flys. With dumbbells in each of my hands, Jack rested his hands under my elbows as I extended my arms upwards until they were parallel with the floor. His waist against mine—his masculinity pressing into my bottom. It was all I could do to breathe through each repetition.

The hour went by quickly and before I knew it I was lying face down on the massage table and Jack was stretching me out. No massage like I fantasized about the day before, just a straight up stretch out to help my muscles recover from the workout he put them through.

"There's something different about you today, Libby," he said. I wasn't my usual chatty self and he'd noticed. He was good like that, always observant.

"My mind is preoccupied with my exhibition."

"That's this week, isn't it? Are you expecting a big crowd?"

Yeah, with one less person now however—that's when it hit me, why not formally invite Jack to join me?

"Would you like to come?" Nice choice of words, Libby.

"That's so kind of you to ask, but the tickets are a bit out of my price range."

Since I didn't know if any of my work would sell, I decided to charge a five-hundred-dollar entrance fee at the door to ensure we donated a minimum amount of money to the charity we were supporting. I had to remember that while Jack charged a premium per hour of his time, five hundred bucks was a steep cover charge. Then I had an epiphany.

"My husband has been called out of town on a business trip. You can have his ticket."

"In that case," Jack said while pushing my legs towards my chin, "how can I say no?"

As he finished stretching me, I closed my eyes and imagined how Thursday would play out—and it's fucking hot.

#

All of my guests have gone home from my exhibition and I'm alone in my gallery cleaning up when, all of a sudden, there's a gentle knock at the door. I turn my head to see Jack dressed in a dark suit that looks as if it was painted on his body. He's holding a bouquet of flowers—tulips, my favorite. I walk over to my door to unlock it and let him in.

"I am so sorry I'm late, Libby," he says as he looks deep into my eyes. I know he's being sincere, those chestnut eyes wouldn't lie to me.

"One of my patients complained of chest pains after our session and I went with her to the hospital. Her son is with her now and I came over as quickly as I could."

As if his bulging muscles weren't enough, Jack Gregory—The Rock of Westport—is also loyal to his clients, so loyal that he would accompany one to the hospital and wait with them.

I didn't want to make him feel bad, so instead of telling him that he missed a great time, I walk him through each piece of art I had on display and tell the story about each.

"Let's start here." I walk him over to a painting I call Horizon's End. "This depicts two people sitting on the beach back to back. You see the sun going down over the horizon, signifying the end of something."

"Their marriage," Jack observes.

"That's right," I confirm and walk him to another.

"This one is called Mirror Mirror. It shows a couple standing in front of a mirror, but their reflections are not of themselves today, but rather who they were when they first met. Each figure in the reflection has a tear in their eye. What does that mean to you, Jack?"

"They are getting a glimpse into their future and don't like what they see."

This man wasn't just a jock, he was an artist at heart.

I walk him through all my other pictures and we finally end on one I call Broken Promises. The painting depicts two people in the throes of sexual intercourse on a bed while a third person in the window looks on with a shocked expression. "What do you see in this one?"

"The woman has stepped out on her husband, he's looking in from the window wondering what he did wrong."

"And what do you think he did wrong?" I ask.

Without hesitation, Jack pulls me close and says, "Leaving you alone for too long," before planting a kiss on my mouth.

Before I know it, he's leading me to the back room of my gallery, towards my office. Once inside, he lifts me up on my desk and reaches under the black cocktail dress I am wearing and pulls down my thong. There's no massage, no teasing, he goes right for what he wants. I lie down on the desk, spread my legs, and he bends down between them and takes me into his mouth, but just for a second— such a tease. He then kisses me up and down my legs, gently caressing my inner thighs with his tongue until I can't take it anymore.

I grab him by the head to press his face against me and start moving my hips in circles. My excitement builds as his tongue presses against my pearl and I almost climax as he slides the tip of his finger inside me and moves it around in circles. The combination of his fluttering tongue and vibrating finger take me over the edge and I release while squeezing his face with my thighs. My body continues to shiver after my orgasm completes.

He comes up for air and I sit up to pull off his shirt—I need him inside me so that we can climax together, but he pulls away.

"Tonight was about you, Libby. Consider that my apology for missing the show."

#

I snapped out of this glorious daydream when I heard my name being called from somewhere far away.

"Libby? Libby, are you okay?"

As I rejoined the land of the conscious, the voice got closer and closer. I had dozed off on the table while Jack was stretching me and got lost in a fantasy.

"I will be," I said and then showed Jack to the door and went upstairs to draw a bath.

CHAPTER ELEVEN
The Fly

So yes, I made the first move and invited Jack to be my guest—more like my date—for my art exhibition. I knew that my intentions definitely weren't pure as evidenced by the fantasy I had while he was stretching me out that Monday morning. I felt it all over my body—I wanted him, badly.

It's time, though, to go thirteen hundred miles south of Westport and back down to Fort Lauderdale to see how Terry's business trip unfolded, and the curveballs he had to hit down there.

#

Pop and I didn't speak a word on the way back to his place that night; I was fuming at the prospect of having my name associated with a drug bust in the morning edition and I could tell he was upset about something too, though he wasn't letting on what it was—ill communication is a family trait passed down from father to son. *It certainly is.*

Once we got to the parking lot of Yasgur's Farm South,

my curiosity got the better of me and I pushed him on it.

"I know why I'm upset, but why are you so glum? Don't tell me no one at this place has any reefer."

"Who the hell calls it reefer anymore?" Pop asked with a smirk. Another thing passed down from father to son, our trademark facial expression.

"Call it whatever you want, Pop, but I just want to know why you are so down."

The man shook his head. "It's getting late and you have a busy day tomorrow. Let's get you settled in a room and maybe we'll talk about it tomorrow, okay?"

My father had just admitted that there was something to talk about, which was a big step in our father/son relationship, but I also knew the man well enough not to push him any further on it.

Pop walked me through the main lobby, introduced me to some of his pals—all of whom smelled like patchouli oil —and then arranged a room for me on the second floor.

"Only the penthouse will do for my son," Pop said to the elderly woman behind the counter. She was as tall as Bea Arthur and had the face of Estelle Getty. She smelled not-so-vaguely of urine, so I nicknamed her the golden shower girl. *Where had his sense of humor been hiding?*

Pop walked me to my room and helped me with my bags. We spoke for a bit in front of the door.

"I have a doctor's appointment in the morning, so can you take one of those Uber things to your office?"

"Sure," I said. "Doctor's appointment?" I asked. To my knowledge, the man hadn't been to a doctor in the past forty years. If he was going to one tomorrow, something must have been wrong.

"Don't worry about it. I'll catch up with you tomorrow

night. There's someone I want you to meet."

"I'm not sure when I'll get back from work. I have no idea what's in store for me."

"If you were a writer, you could make your own hours," my father reminded me.

"But I'm not a writer, Pop. I'm a lawyer."

"Alright, your honor, the defense rests. See you tomorrow, and don't think about leaving here for the Hilton or I'll hold you in contempt of court."

Pop left and I could hear him coughing as he walked down the steps back to the first floor. Something wasn't right, but he wasn't ready to tell me what it was.

I turned the key that Pop gave me to unlock the door, that's right, a physical key—not one of those plastic cards with a magnetic strip—and entered the room where I was going to spend the next few evenings.

The smell of eucalyptus was an assault to my olfactory sense that was only eclipsed by the visuals in the room; there was no door to the bathroom, rather strings of beads hung down as if the decor was inspired by Greg Brady's attic apartment. *Do you think he banged his stepsister up there?* The nightstand next to my bed was furnished with a lava lamp and there was no television to be found on the wall —my only option for entertainment was a book called *The Road to Woodstock* by Michael Lang. Above my bed hung a poster of David Crosby as he looked in 1968, complete with receding hair, trademark mustache, and growing gut.

I put my stuff down, freshened up in the bathroom, and then lay down on the bed and tried to get some sleep, but was kept up by the sounds of people on either side of my room having sex. I once heard that venereal diseases ran rampant in retirement communities and if what I heard through the walls of my room at Yasgur's Farm South was any indication of what went on in similar places, I understood why.

I moved onto my side, placed two pillows over my ear to mute the noise, and went to sleep.

The next morning, I woke up early and went for a run down a road called the Galt Ocean Mile. This stretch of road runs parallel to the beach and includes some of Fort Lauderdale's most expensive housing—a far cry from where I grew up out west in the modest town of Plantation.

As I ran, I tried to mentally prepare myself for the next three days and wondered what Paul would have me doing. Preston had assigned all of my current workload to one of his other senior associates as I was supposed to be at Paul's beck and call for the next three days. I'd heard he was eccentric, but I had no idea just how different he was—all I heard were the rumors.

Some who'd met him said he had been married to the same woman for twenty years but that he was a known philanderer. Others had told me he suffered from a rare eye disease that forced him to wear dark sunglasses, even while indoors. Another rumor was that he lost a six-figure bet when he took the under on the number of women who would come forward to expose Tiger Woods as a sex freak. *Sounds like a quality guy.*

After I got back to Yasgur's, I took a lukewarm shower —not by choice, mind you—got dressed, and then arranged for an Uber to take me to the office, which is located on the corner of Oakland Park Boulevard and Bayview, right over the Intracoastal Waterway.

While most top firms made their homes along

downtown Fort Lauderdale's skyline, mine was housed in a small building near the water. Our offices in Connecticut were in a more traditional space, but when Paul decided to move down to Fort Lauderdale, he wanted something with views of the water. Plus, while it was technically our headquarters because the boss was there, for all intents and purposes, it was really a satellite office with a skeleton crew.

Once I walked in the door, I was greeted by Nicole Robinson, Paul's executive assistant and the firm's first employee. Most of the associates have never had any direct contact with Paul, myself included. All communication from him came from Nicole, who many of us referred to as Mrs. Robinson due to the rumors that she once had an affair with a summer associate half her age.

That morning she was wearing a red dress that flattered her tall and slender figure. Her blonde hair fell just to her shoulders and her lack of wrinkles suggested that, although a resident of the Sunshine State, Mrs. Robinson wasn't a sun worshiper. I could easily see why a young guy would have been thrilled to spend an evening with her.

"Good morning, Mr. Gardner," Mrs. Robinson said while extending her hand. She was strictly business. "Mr. Hewson is expecting you. Right this way."

I followed her down the hallway. She walked down the hall as if she was leading a platoon in a morning march and then stopped abruptly in front of a large door on which she knocked three times—two in quick succession and a third two beats later. From the other side I heard the same pattern and then Mrs. Robinson pushed opened the door and I laid my eyes on Paul Hewson for the first time.

Wait for it.

Standing in front of me was a man who I towered over. I'm not a tall guy—on a good day I'm 5'10"—but Paul only came up to my chest. I guessed he was a good five inches shorter than me. He didn't wear a suit, rather he wore black designer jeans and a ratty tee-shirt covered up by an unzipped leather jacket. He wore black army boots on his feet, and as I looked down at his head, I noticed his hair was pulled backward but that his hairline was a bit too perfect—clearly had plugs. On his face was two-day-old salt and pepper stubble. Capping off this rock-star look were his trademark dark sunglasses.

I had a hard time believing this guy was a golf fanatic —he looked like the type who'd make fun of such a traditional game.

"I'm pleased to meet you, Terry Gardner," he said with a slight hint of an Irish accent. I went to shake his hand, but he pushed mine aside.

"I'm a hugger, Terry Gardner."

His hug lasted a few beats too long and, given our difference in height, I felt as if we were slow dancing to the last song at a middle school dance. *"In Your Eyes"?*

"Let's have a seat, shall we, Terry Gardner?" This was the third time he'd used both my first and last name—I wondered how long that would last.

"Great," I said.

We didn't sit down on the couch in his office, though, or the chairs in front of his desk. We sat on the floor, Indian-style. *Maybe I was wrong about him.*

"So my six apostles tell me they are split on whether or not you've got what it takes to make partner." *Nope.*

The six apostles he spoke of were the firm's senior

partners—I'd heard Paul had a God complex, but I didn't know how far he took it.

"That's correct, but let me just say…"

Paul raised his hand in the air and squeezed his fingers into a fist to suggest that I stop talking. I did.

"It's up to me to see if you have what it takes. I've read your file and by all accounts you are an exemplary employee and an eagle lawyer, so my goal this week is to see what kind of man Terry Gardner is. The jump from senior associate to partner will change your life and we are very, very selective about who gets to make that leap."

I looked at him and wondered if it was my time to talk.

"Speak your mind, Terry Gardner."

"Sir…"

"Please, call me Paul."

"Paul, I just want you to know that I'll do whatever it takes to…"

His fist went up again.

"Your ambition has been noted, Terry Gardner. All partners at this firm have it and you wouldn't be sitting in this office if you didn't. Ambition alone won't make the difference, your character will, and that is what I will be assessing over the next few days."

My character? How was he planning on doing that by sitting in an office with me?

"I understand that you were born and raised here in South Florida. Let's go take a drive to your old neighborhood in Plantation and take a walk."

Before I could respond, Paul was up on his feet and walking toward the door.

"Nicole, please tell Jenna that I'm walking to the car."

"Where shall I tell her you are going?" Mrs. Robinson

asked.

"Plantation," Paul replied.

When she heard his answer, Mrs. Robinson made a face suggesting she didn't care much for my hometown.

"Come now, Terry Gardner, my driver will take us," he said, and I followed him to the garage where a tall and slender twenty-something brunette wearing a belly shirt and cutoff shorts met us standing next to a stretch limousine.

"Jenna Tufts, meet Terry Gardner. Terry Gardner, meet Jenna Tufts." She was unlike any limo driver I'd ever seen —she looked more like an extra from an '80s music video than your typical formal livery pilot.

I extended my hand, but Jenna came in to give me a hug. She smelled of lavender, but it wasn't her scent that distracted me, it was the feeling of her breasts being pushed against my chest that caused me to lose concentration. I could tell that she wasn't wearing a bra— God I missed South Florida. *Note to self, ditch the bra.*

"Jenna, take us to 841 North West 67th Avenue in Plantation."

Paul knew the address of my childhood home. I wonder what else he knew about me.

The drive to Plantation took about thirty minutes and Paul spent the entire time on the phone; I spent my time responding to emails and sneaking glances at our chauffeur. I considered tapping out a text to Libby but decided against it. She was so upset the night before last that I knew texting wasn't a smart idea. I decided I'd call her later when I had some privacy. *My phone never rang.*

Jenna turned onto my old street and I was shocked at how little it had changed in the twenty years since I'd left home. My father had sold our home when he bought Yasgur's and the new owners hadn't changed much.

"Home sweet home, Terry Gardner," Paul said and then got out of the car. I did the same.

"Tell me the first thing that comes to mind when you look at the house you were born in."

I wasn't expecting such a deep question and it took me a minute to come up with an answer. Finally I said, "Happiness."

"Why happiness?" Paul asked.

"We didn't have much when I grew up, but there was always laughter in my home."

"Laughter is a good thing, Terry Gardner. Do you still have laughter in your home?"

Was this guy a lawyer or was he Dr. Phil? Although I was hesitant to admit it, I had to reply, "No."

"That's unfortunate," he said, and then we walked around the block. It was the middle of the morning, so few people were outside—had it been the summertime back in the 1980s, every kid in the neighborhood would have been outside on their bikes or splashing around in a pool. As we walked around the block, it was quiet.

"You have three siblings, Terry Gardner. Are you close?"

"They still live down here and I'm up in Connecticut," I replied. "So we don't get together all that often."

"Distance shouldn't have anything to do with it. All of my family is in Ireland, but I still consider us close," he replied.

Last night, when walking around Pompano Beach with Pop, I started to realize how much of a shame it was that I didn't keep in touch with my siblings, and now Paul was making me feel bad about that.

"Family is the most important thing in the world," he said. "Friends and lovers come and go, but family will stay with you forever. Never forget that, Terry Gardner."

We had made one revolution around my old block and were now standing back in front of my childhood home. The current owner was now outside trimming some hedges.

"When was the last time you were in your old home, Terry Gardner?"

"Pop sold it five years ago. I came to help him move."

"Let's have a look inside."

I started to protest, "We can't just…" but he paid me no attention and walked up to the owner.

"Pardon me," he said. "But that guy over there grew up here and was hoping to have a look inside."

The woman to whom he was speaking looked like a deer in headlights as the rock-star-looking founder of my law firm spoke to her. He must have said something to warm her heart, because all concern dropped from her face and she welcomed us into my old home.

The front door led right to an open room; on one side there was a dining room table and on the other there was a living area complete with sectional couch and a flatscreen TV that hung over a faux fireplace. When I was a kid, my mother and father, when they were still together, threw legendary poker parties in this room and the air would be thick with smoke. As I walked through the room I could almost smell the scent of stale cigarettes.

"Take me to your bedroom," Paul said.

I walked down a short hallway and we passed my sister's room on the left and my brother's room on the right. The room I shared with my brother Jimmy was at the end of the hall. When we entered it, I had the sense that I'd just walked through a time warp. I could almost see Jimmy and me lying in our twin beds and passing a ball to each other—which was something we would do frequently.

"I lost you for a moment, Terry Gardner. Where did you go?"

"Sorry," I apologized. "Being in here got me to thinking about my brother Jimmy. We shared this room."

"When was the last time you spoke with him?"

"Five years ago, the last time I was here."

"I think you should change that this week, Terry Gardner."

"I don't think there will be time to see him, or any of my siblings for that matter."

"Of course there will be," Paul said. "I'm giving you tomorrow off to do just that."

What he just said had caught me off guard. I was supposed to be down here so that he could evaluate whether or not I was worthy to become a partner in the firm, not take a walk down memory lane. This was the strangest interview ever and I had no idea whether I was passing or failing.

"I think we have overstayed our welcome," Paul said and then led me out of the room. He thanked the current owner for letting us in and then we got back into the limo and went back to the office. He made call after call the entire time.

When we got back to the office he informed me that he had to spend time working the entire afternoon and that we'd regroup Thursday morning at his golf course.

"Jenna here will take you back to where you are staying," Paul said and then got out of the car. He was a man full of contradictions: rock-star look, sentimental personality, but one hundred percent shark when he was on the phone talking business. I had no idea where I stood in his mind.

"Where to, Mr. Gardner?" Jenna asked.

"Just Terry," I replied and then gave her the address to my pop's place.

"This is…interesting…" Jenna said when she pulled up in front of Yasgur's Farm South.

"You don't know the half of it," I replied and then thanked her for the ride.

CHAPTER TWELVE

Laughter Backfires

To say that I was shocked when I first read Terry's account of his first full day in Florida would have been an understatement. That the founding partner of his firm took him on a trip of his childhood in order to assess his character caught me completely off guard—of course I didn't know anything about that last year when it happened.

I was still seething inside about Terry's decision to head down to Florida the week of my art exhibition and apparently wasn't doing a great job of hiding that fact from everyone who came into the gallery that Tuesday. More than one person asked me what was bothering me and no fewer than three customers told me that I should smile more.

I heard the door open and was surprised to see Marley walk through it late in the afternoon as I knew she flew to Chicago the day before, but then remembered she said she was only going away overnight.

"Hey, chica," she said as she walked into the gallery and

approached the counter I was standing behind.

"Listen, something has been bothering me since Sunday and I didn't want to say this over the phone. I'm sorry about pushing you at the Duck. I had no right to tell you how to deal with your Terry issues and clearly overstepped my bounds."

I had been holding a grudge against Marley since Sunday because I did think she was a little heavy-handed with the way she spoke to me and was relieved that she offered an apology. It pained me to be mad at her.

I came out from behind the counter and gave her a hug. "Thanks," I said while patting her on the back.

"You look down," she said, and then I told her how Terry had to take a sudden trip to Florida that week.

"I'm sorry, chica, but maybe he'll make it back."

"And maybe you will become submissive."

"You know me too well. Hey, tonight at Yuck Yucks they are doing an open mic night and I'm on the list, come with me. I'm trying some new material and it looks as if you could use a good laugh."

Yuck Yucks was the nickname for our town's aging comedy club. The actual name was Ha Ha's, but everyone called it Yuck Yucks because the food made dorm food taste appetizing. I once saw a box in the dumpster outside of the club that was marked *Grade D but edible.*

Marley is a woman of contradictions, a total Dom in the bedroom, but she has a sense of humor as if she were the offspring of Artie Lange and Amy Schumer—not that I'd want to picture them in the act of procreation. She'd been doing open mics at the club for years and was pretty popular with regulars.

"I don't know, there's so much to do to prepare for

Thursday," I protested, offering a weak argument.

Marley looked around the gallery and saw that it was basically all set up for the event.

"You've gotta do better than that, chica. Give me twenty good reasons why you can't go tonight."

"Twenty?"

Marley smiled and I relented.

"Okay, but I want to be home by ten, and you're driving."

"Chica, I'm off tomorrow. We'll take an Uber."

#

Tuesday night is not a big night for Westport's nightlife scene and our comedy club is the only place that gets any kind of crowd. While it books national headliners from Wednesday through Sunday, it reserves Tuesday as an open mic night to support local talent.

As Marley and I walked in, it was hard to avoid the smell of stale beer and crushed dreams as we entered the main room after paying the nominal cover charge. As I walked across the floor, I noticed that it was sticky and wasn't brave enough to ask why. We were seated at a table towards the front of the stage.

Those selected for an open mic spot have only five minutes of stage time, so they have to bring their real A game for their set, which of course doesn't mean much because most are people who have never been on stage before and don't know how to work a crowd. Every now and then, though, someone comes up and just knocks it out of the park, and I was hoping we'd get lucky that night, though the woman performing on stage wasn't getting it done and left before her five minutes were even up. Our waitress came over once the stage was empty.

"My name is Vanessa and it's my pleasure to serve you tonight. I just want to remind you that there is a two drink minimum. What would you like?"

I'm a wine girl through and through, but I wouldn't trust whatever they poured at Yuck Yucks, so opted for a vodka soda with a splash of cranberry.

"Same," Marley said.

"I'll be right back with those. Do you care for anything to nibble on tonight?"

I looked at Marley and had to suppress a laugh. The only reason to eat at Yuck Yucks was if you were looking to lose ten pounds quickly from a stomach bug.

"I think we'll stick with drinks," Marley said, and Vanessa walked towards her next victims.

I was about to say something to Marley when the emcee's voice came booming over the club's PA system. "Ladies and gentlemen, if you've ever ridden our Metro North train into Manhattan you might recognize our next performer. Give it up for Larry the Conductor.

I knew Larry back from the days I spent commuting to New York when I worked in advertising. He would play his trademark harmonica whenever he entered a car on the train to start collecting tickets. He wasn't very good at playing the thing—certainly no one would mistake him for John Popper of Blues Traveler—but he did have something that the other conductors lacked, a personality.

A moment after taking the stage, our ears were assaulted by a series of notes that weren't meant to be played in sequence together.

"Good evening, ladies and gentlemen, last month I won an award for best conductor on the New Haven Line." He paused and waited for the inevitable round of applause the handful of people in the club would give him. "Do you know how I got so good?" he asked after accepting their praise.

"How?" four people asked in unison.

"A lot of training!" he said and then blew into the harmonica.

"The other day I'm walking through the train collecting tickets and I pause in front of a guy having a full-on breakfast. Eggs, toast, potatoes, you name it. I looked at him and said, 'Well it looks like someone found the chew-chew train.'" The harmonica blared again.

He spent the next four minutes telling train-based jokes and I spent them looking for Vanessa because I really needed my drink. She finally came when Larry left the stage; Marley and I said cheers, and we each took a sip.

"When do you go up?" I asked, wondering how long I'd have to sit through the evening's talent.

"After the break," Marley responded.

"Now, ladies and gentlemen, put your hands together and welcome Tyler O'Danger to the stage."

"He's cute," Marley said.

She was right. With blond hair that fell to his shoulders and a broad set of shoulders that looked as if he could press a smart car over his head, Tyler was likely the hunkiest guy to ever grace the Yuck Yucks stage. Unfortunately, it all went to shit when he opened his mouth.

"My name is Tyler and I'm a student at Staples high school here in Westport," he said with a voice that was no fewer than three octaves too high for his appearance. "I smoke a lot of weed. I guess that's why they call it high school."

No one in the club laughed and I kind of felt bad for the kid, so I looked at him and smiled. This was a bad idea because one thing I've learned about comics is that whenever they are bombing and see a friendly face, they will try to engage.

"Hey, check out the milfs in the front here. Alright, either of you want to go home with a guy whose voice is too high?"

This act of self-deprecation earned a few laughs from the club's small crowd.

"Seriously, maybe one of you has a kid my age and he could become my stepson. I could teach him how to be a man, you know, I've got all the cheat codes for *Grand Theft Auto 4*."

This earned him some more laughs.

"Seriously, why don't you come back with me to my place tonight? My mom goes to bed early and I'll give you the best two and a half minutes you've had all week."

This too earned some laughter, but I was getting tired of being the focus of his attention and fortunately his five minutes were just about up.

"I bet I could teach him a thing or two," Marley said to me after he left the stage.

"I'm sure you could," I agreed. I started to loosen up and have fun and found that laughing made me feel better.

"Terry call you today?"

"No, but I didn't expect him to. He was supposed to be spending the entire day with his firm's founder. Guessing he's still at work as we speak."

"Okay, no more Terry talk," Marley said.

"Ladies and gentlemen, we have an extra-special treat for you tonight. Here at Ha Ha's we are excited to welcome a famous actor and new Westport resident to the stage. You know him as Kyle Dixon from the 1980s hit drama *Casa Grande*, please put your hands together for Blaze Hazelwood.

Marley looked at me and smiled. The two of us grew up watching *Casa Grande* every Thursday night. Blaze was the hottest TV star in the world at the time but kind of faded away after that. Rumor has it he starred in a production of *Back to the Future: The Musical*, which bombed so hard on Broadway that everyone associated with it imploded afterwards.

"Well this is exciting," Marley said.

"He still looks fine," I offered.

"Thank you for that warm welcome, kind people of Westport," Blaze said, with just a hint of an English accent. I'd read somewhere that he adopted it shortly after Madonna started speaking with one—they'd apparently met at a party once and Blaze considered her a bestie (I'll admit to having an unhealthy obsession with the man ever since I was a kid in the '80s).

"Anyone here on Facebook?" Blaze asked, after which the crowd responded by clapping their hands. "Me too. Though something awkward happened to me on it. My first luv tracked me down and friended me. I'm single and was curious to see what she looked like, so I accepted the request. She then sends me a note asking if I remember the first time we had sex. Now this is a girl I haven't spoken to in almost thirty years and she jumps right to sex talk. Who does she think she is? How would I remember such a thing?"

Blaze then took out his phone and pretended to type on it while saying, "Of course I do. Your parents were out of town and—" He cuts himself off as a way of inviting the audience to laugh and it worked—he was as charismatic as ever.

Blaze addressed the crowd again, "The first time is always awkward, isn't it?" The audience responded by clapping.

"Mine was extra awkward because, even though I came of age in Hollywood, I was born on a farm in upstate New York and my parents were very simple people. They didn't talk to me about sex, hell they didn't even teach me the proper name for my private parts. I didn't have a dick, I had a po po," Blaze said and raised his eyebrows. The crowd laughed.

He then touched his butt. "This wasn't an ass, it was a coolie." The crowd laughed again.

"So that night I'm trying to play it cool with my girl. I put a little George Michael on the record player and cozied on up to her. We started making out and things were getting heavy. She asked me what I wanted, so I whispered into her ear, "I want you to take my po po in your mouth!"

Blaze said this by whispering into the mic and the crowd roared with laughter; Blaze himself couldn't keep himself from giggling.

"When we were finally doing it and I was on top of her, she asked me again what I wanted, so I told her to spank my coolie." Someone behind laughed so hard they almost snarfed their drink all over my back.

"I realized that she was the one taking the lead, so I asked her what she wanted." Blaze paused and then whispered into the microphone. "Play with my jellybean."

The club's patrons club gave him a standing ovation.

"I wonder if he's a sub," Marley whispered to me as Blaze walked off the stage. We sat back down when the emcee returned.

"We are just going to take a fifteen-minute break before we start up again. If you want to join us on stage, we have a few open slots left at the end of the night. I want to remind you that there is a two drink minimum and all appetizers are now half price." As the emcee said this, he shook his head, warning the audience not to fall for the trap the club's manager just laid.

When the emcee left the stage, we flagged down Vanessa and ordered two more drinks.

"This was a good idea," I said.

"Told ya," Marley agreed.

"Though I'm not supposed to be drinking during the week. Jack says it's a big no-no."

"Your trainer is the fun police. Cut the carbs, cut the alcohol…those are my two favorite food groups!"

Marley had a great delivery, she was a natural comedian. "You ready to go up there?" I asked.

"I'm nervous, but I have some good stuff to try out," she replied.

A few moments later, the emcee was back. "Ladies and gentlemen, give a warm round of applause to your favorite local, Marley Carlin."

Marley got up from her chair and walked to the stage and grabbed the microphone. She took a deep breath and then started talking to the crowd.

"I want to buy a hospice center," she said, and everyone looked around nervously. Who the hell starts a comedy set with a hospice joke?

"You heard me right, I want to buy a hospice center

and then tear it down. And then I want to build a bar on top of the grounds of that former hospice center and I want to name the bar The Pulled Plug."

This comment caught everyone off guard and people started to laugh.

"And we are going to have different drink specials every night of the week. Like Mondays we'll have a drink called *I See the Light*, which will of course be tequila based. Tuesdays we'll serve up our signature drink *CPR*, one part Campari, one part Patrón, and one rum, and 100% guaranteed to make you wish you were dead. Wednesdays, of course, we'll feature *The End of the Line*, which is a shot of Jägermeister along with pulled pork sliders, catered by Yuck Yucks of course."

The crowd howled.

Marley took a sip of water and then continued, "I was in Chicago yesterday and I happened to walk by an orphanage located across the street from an Olive Garden restaurant and it got me wondering, can orphans eat at a family restaurant?"

The crowd was hysterical; Marley was really killing up there.

"My doctor is a real downer. I'm a girl who likes to have a lot of sex and I'll admit it, I don't use protection all the time, so after he lectured me for the sixty-ninth time about this I stopped him and said, 'Doc, you only live once, right?'

"'No,' he replied. 'You live every day, you only die once.'"

The crowed laughed in unison again. Where did she come up with this stuff?

"But it's true what I said, I do like sex. Love it. And

apologies to any of my sisters out there who may not appreciate the male form and prefer to make every night pink taco night, but I love a good dick."

Everyone started to clap when she said this. She had them all captivated.

"I don't even mind blowing a guy's dick so long as he returns the favor, you know what I mean, ladies?"

The women in the crowd started hooting and hollering.

"But, guys, let me learn you something here. There's a big difference between getting a blowjob and fucking a woman in the face. Calm the jets a bit, will ya, jeez."

She really had them going.

"Now I'm not married and I refuse to share my personal space with anyone, so I don't have access to a house dick. I have a friend, though, whose husband has a great fucking dick. She used to tell me that it was so big she thought his dick had a dick. If that kind of dick were attached to my man, I wouldn't let it leave the house. I'd be like, 'Okay, Terry, you can go out, but your dick has to stay here. I don't trust you out in public with that thing. I'll just sit here and read a book with your dick while you go bowling with the guys.'"

Everyone in the club was hysterical, but she was talking about my husband and I didn't appreciate how much time she'd obviously spent thinking about his cock.

"My name is Marley Carlin, thanks for being so great."

Just as the crowd had done with Blaze, they all stood up and gave Marley a round of applause.

"What did you think of my new material?" I could tell Marley was exhilarated, but inside I was red with anger. "What's the matter?"

"You just did two minutes on my husband's dick."

"That's more than you've done on it in the past few months," she said, trying to funnel the energy she attained from her stage high and keep the jokes coming.

I didn't find it funny and got up to leave.

"Hey, the night is still young and you haven't finished your second drink."

"Stay as long as you want," I told her. "I'm taking an Uber home."

When she got up to follow me out, Marley was intercepted by the club's owner, who propositioned her to take an opening spot for this Friday's show. Seeing that she was now engaged in some kind of negotiation, I whipped out my phone and arranged for a car to take me home.

CHAPTER THIRTEEN
Reunion

It turns out that Wednesday was a pivotal day for both me and Terry—one year later and I still can't believe how that night ended for him, and how that impacted The Event. I'll share his story now and then reveal what I learned about myself that day. You might be missing my snarky comments in this reflection of Terry's; I just didn't have it in me to make them in this part of his reflection.

\#

When I got back to Pop's place late in the afternoon on Tuesday, he was nowhere to be found. I tried calling him, but he didn't answer his phone. I asked around for him, but either no one had seen him, or they weren't willing to divulge his hiding spot—I assumed he was stoned somewhere.

Without anything to do, I grabbed some takeout for dinner and called it an early night. I woke up Wednesday morning to the sound of thumping coming from my door; I opened it to see Pop standing in the doorway looking like death warmed over.

"You look like shit," I remarked.

"It's good to see you too. I came to see if you needed a ride to work."

I explained to Pop the unorthodox day I had with Paul and that he gave me the day off, suggesting I spend some time with my siblings. The look of surprise on Pop's face resembled that on a man getting a prostate exam for the first time.

"That's actually perfect," he said.

"How so?"

"They are all coming here for dinner tonight. I told them that you were in town and that you wanted to see them. You should do a better job of keeping in touch with them, you know."

"Phones work both ways, Pop," I retorted.

"Yeah, but you are the connector, Terry, always were. You were the one who always got us together and they came to rely on you for that. I'm not saying they're right, but when you were younger you spoiled them."

Pop was right. Out of the four Gardner siblings, I arranged every family get-together, and even when I'd stayed in the northeast after college, I initiated all contact.

"Now that you have the day off, I'll tell them to come earlier."

If Pop was excited about all of us being together, his body language and tone of voice weren't buying it.

"What's the matter, Pop?" I asked.

"Later," he said. "Come on down to my room, there's something I want to give you."

"I should probably put on some pants first," I said.

Pop looked down and saw that I was standing in my boxer shorts.

"Yeah, if they ladies get a look at you in your skivvies, they are likely to pounce. There's a shortage of men here."

I got dressed and followed Pop down the stairs and to his room and found it to be remarkably organized. He'd always been a pack rat and I was surprised at how well he kept up with it. That said, it still smelled like stale weed.

"I'm impressed, Pop. Place looks good, smells like shit but looks good."

He just turned around and offered a smirk suggesting I drop the topic. As he walked over to his bookshelf, I noticed that his pants had started to fall down and that he looked even thinner than he did when he picked me up from the airport on Monday night.

"I've been doing some spring cleaning and came across these."

He handed me a number of black marble composition notebooks—the ones I kept in high school and college. "You kept these?"

"Of course. I'm cleaning out some stuff and wanted to make sure you got them back. There's some good stuff in there."

"You read them?" I said with an angry tone.

"I found them in a box of stuff that you didn't take back to Connecticut with you. I was curious."

"They were private!" I protested.

"You should have kept them then."

"I don't believe this."

"What I don't believe, Terry," Pop said while pointing into my chest, "is how you can be so goddamned stupid. You were a talented writer and instead of following your passion, you are out there chasing the almighty dollar."

Have I mentioned the fact that he hated my being a lawyer?

"Well, Pop, that's easy for you to say seeing that you've won the lottery and all. The rest of us have to work. I want to provide a stable life for my kids."

"What kids?" Pop asked. "You are forty-one years old and childless."

"We are going to try once I become a partner."

"Which will be when? This week? Next month? Next year? You can't plan your life's events around work, son. What are you putting first?"

"Oh, what, am I supposed to take advice from a guy who never outgrew the sixties? You never put anyone but yourself first, Pop."

I didn't realize how much anger I had towards my father until he started questioning my own priorities.

"You know, you're right, Terry. I was a selfish underachiever who didn't take anything seriously and skated through life, that's all fair. And there's a lot I regret about that. But I'm an old man now and there isn't time for me to go back and change what I've done. But you still have time, son.

Agreeing to stay down here was a bad idea and I silently contemplated how I'd get back at Libby for calling my dad.

"Now I have to lie down for a bit," Pop said. "Your siblings are coming around three and we are going to grill down by the beach."

I followed him into his bedroom and watched him lie down on the bed. He looked so lonely in that California king-sized monstrosity, and as I considered how old and tired he seemed, I felt bad for blowing up at him.

"I've got some time to kill, do you want me to go to Publix and pick up some food?" It was my way of extending a peace offering.

"Thank you for asking, but I'm sending my friend Sol out for food. You should go back to your room and reacquaint yourself with the old Terry Gardner. Maybe you'll find he was a pretty good guy."

I looked at the books I held in my hand and admitted to myself that maybe the emotions I'd been experiencing, particularly the anger I directed towards Pop, were based in the fear I had at the thought of rediscovering who I was.

"I'll see you later, Pop."

He didn't hear me, he was already asleep.

#

I went back to my room with nothing planned. I considered going to play golf, but the weather changed on a dime; it was sunny five minutes ago, but now thunderheads had rolled in and a big storm was looming just off shore. At the first flash of lightning followed by a loud crack of thunder, I took a seat on the couch and started reading through my old journals.

After going through all the sappy stuff I'd written in high school, I opened the journal I kept in college and turned to a dog-eared page in one I kept my senior year.

June 15th, 1997. My Everything

Tonight I stared into my future. Libby Anderson has captured my heart and soul and tonight we consummated our love for one another by becoming one person, one body, one heart.

When I was inside her, I felt complete—as if all of my fears had melted away and she became my everything. No other woman has ever had this kind of effect on me—it's been an hour since we stopped making love and I'm wide awake with restlessness. The thought of her has taken over my mind and I want nothing more than to take her again so that I may feel that completeness, that comfort, that passion —but she looks so sweet sleeping, I dare not wake her.

I know I'm only twenty-one years old and that she's barely eighteen, but I'm going to marry this girl. I'm not going to let her get away and I am going to prove to her that she is my everything. I'll never let her slip away, I'll take care of her and we will be together, forever, world without end, Amen.

I re-read it multiple times that afternoon and wondered whether I lived up to the promise I'd made twenty years ago. Sure, we were going through a rough patch, but at the time I thought that would be over soon. Still, reading that promise stirred something in me that wasn't there before I went down to Florida—something was happening inside me, but I didn't know what it was.

I realized I hadn't called her since I'd been down to Florida, not that she called me either, but that trip down memory lane encouraged me to pick up the phone and reach out—my call went straight to voicemail.

I found myself emotionally drained after spending a few hours reading my old journals and decided to take a page out of Pop's playbook and take a nap. For the second time that day, I was awoken by a pounding sound coming from my door. I opened it to find my siblings, Greg, Mia, and Jimmy waiting for me. Greg, the eldest of us, was holding a bottle of Jägermeister.

"Fuck," I said.

"You haven't spoken with us in five years and that's the first thing you say?" Mia asked.

"Good to see you too, sis," I replied.

"Can we go to the beach now?" Jimmy asked. "I'm

hungry."

"Is it still raining?"

"How long have you been asleep for? It stopped raining two hours ago," Greg replied. "Now quit being a fucking pussy and let's get going." He always had a way with words.

I grabbed a baseball cap and followed them out the door, down the stairs, and we walked towards the gate that led to the beach. As we walked, I saw Pop talking to an older, leather-skinned gentleman wearing a Tommy Bahama shirt. As I got closer to the grill they were standing in front of, the air became polluted with the smell of lighter fluid.

"Stand back, Sol," Pop said and threw a match into the grill and shouted, "fire in the hole."

Flames shot three feet into the air and a plume of black smoke hit us all in the face. If it were from weed instead of charcoal we'd all be thoroughly baked.

Greg wasted no time getting the party started and passed around shots of Jäger. I've never liked it as that thick green madness always triggered a gag reflex in me, but not doing one wasn't an option. I chased mine with a beer and then sat down in one of the chairs placed in a circle on the sand.

"Now this is a dream come true, all of my kids together having a party on Wednesday. If only your mother were around to see this."

"She's not dead, Pop," Mia said. "She lives in Naples."

"You know what I mean, Mary Christine." Mia wasn't her given name; it was a nickname she earned from my older brother as he wasn't able to pronounce Mary correctly when they were kids, opting for the simpler Mia.

My father was smiling from ear to ear—whatever had been troubling him before seemed to have passed.

"So Terry," Mia said, "fill your siblings in on what you've been up to over the past five years."

The woman knew how to dish out guilt. It was a trait inherited from our mother's side of the family.

"Yeah, you still married?" Jim asked.

"Why would you even ask that?" I replied, a little ticked off.

Jimmy didn't miss a beat. "Because you haven't had sex with your wife in one hundred and two days."

"What the fuck?" My father's friend Sol spoke up for the first time. Up until then I thought he was a mute.

"What's this nonsense about Terrence?" my father asked.

"How the hell did you know that, Jimmy?'

"I spoke with Robbie the other day," he replied. "He calls me regularly, unlike someone else I know."

Robbie had met Jimmy at my wedding and the two hit it off like long-lost friends.

"Robbie should keep his fucking mouth shut."

Greg handed me another shot of Jäger, which I downed. The second one went down much easier than the first.

"We are going through a rough patch," I said. "We'll be fine."

"I'm not so sure," Sol chimed in again.

"Who are you anyway?" I asked.

"I'm sorry, kids. Allow me to introduce you to Sol Goldstein, my best friend down here. He's a teacher of sorts."

"Oh really," I said sarcastically, "what do you teach?

How to not mind your business?"

"I'm not the person you should be angry at," Sol said. "It's not my fault you are not schtupping your wife."

"Well, it's not my fault either," I argued.

"Don't be so sure," he said while pointing a finger in the air. "How different you are from your old man here. He's schtupped every woman at this place at least three times. The man's got a rod like Moses's staff, blessed by G-d if you ask me."

As he said this, he patted my father on the back. Some things you can't unsee.

"Come find me before the end of the night, I'll give you some good advice."

"Is anybody hungry?" I said as an attempt to change the subject.

"I think I lost my appetite," Mia replied.

Jimmy spoke next. "When do you leave for Connecticut, Terry? I'd love to have you over to see the kids."

Out of the four of us, Jimmy and I were closest in age. They called us Irish twins because we were born eleven months apart; him in January and me in November. Greg was almost ten years my senior and Mia was eight; Jimmy and I had more in common since we were much closer in age.

"I have to go back tomorrow night. Libby has an art exhibition and I am trying to get back for it."

"Trying?" Mia said. "Don't you have a flight back?"

"No," I said. "It all depends on when my golf match with the owner of my firm ends. He's a bit... unpredictable."

I hoped to God that we'd be done with our match by

two so that I could get to the airport by three and on a four o'clock flight back.

"Hey," Greg said. "I'd like to make a toast."

"This should be good," I replied while accepting another shot of Jäger from him.

"To my father and youngest brother, for the appearance they made in the *Sun Sentinel* today!"

"Hear, hear," everyone said and threw their shot down —everyone except me.

"What are you talking about?" I asked.

"Looks like the old man is a bad influence on you, Terry. Trying to buy weed on Pompano Beach. Shame, shame," he said while pretending to ring a bell as a reference to a famous scene in the show *Game of Thrones*.

Why was that in the *Sun Sentinel*? I figured it would only be in the *Pompano Beach Gazette*. I had no idea whether or not Paul Hewson shared Preston's opinion on marijuana, but if he did I was screwed.

"Fucking mayor," Pop said. "Just another attack on the hippies."

"But I'm not a hippie!" I protested.

I had a hard time thinking about anything else that evening and thought that it couldn't possibly get any worse. I was wrong.

CHAPTER FOURTEEN

The First Time

So that was part of Terry's Wednesday (more to come). Now, here's what my day was like.

I woke up that Wednesday morning convinced that that my life was hitting a low point; my husband was down in Florida chasing his almighty partnership, and the night before, I confirmed a suspicion I had since Sunday that my best friend had the hots for my husband. On top of that, the pull I felt towards another man was becoming increasingly stronger; I was convinced that Jack could turn my melancholy existence around—that somehow he held the key to unlock my happiness and fill the void that had been missing in my life.

I checked my phone to see whether or not I had any appointments that day as I open the gallery for appointments only on Wednesdays and was relieved to see I didn't. I allowed myself a smile as I thought of the hour I'd spend with my trainer that morning, but just as the butterflies were starting to flutter in my stomach at the thought of being alone with that muscular specimen of

Jack Gregory, my phone buzzed with a text from the man of the hour himself—think of the devil and he doth appear.

J: Sorry to do this last minute, but I have to cancel this morning. Personal emergency.

Personal emergency? I was having my own personal emergency! I pulled the covers over my head and almost cried; my hour with Jack was the only thing I'd had to look forward to that day.

L: You can make it up to me tomorrow night.

J: Of course. Can't wait.

Well at least I had his presence at my show to look forward to. While my motivation level had dropped to zero, I knew that I had to drag myself out of bed and do something constructive with my time or else I'd waste the day away feeling sorry for myself, and decided that after breakfast I would do some sketching.

When I was in college, I took a seminar from a licensed psychologist who used art as a therapeutic instrument for helping her patients uncover the subconscious ways they saw, and subsequently felt about, themselves.

She would have her patients think of a specific scenario and then draw themselves in that setting; after they were done she would probe on specific elements such as the meaningfulness of the chosen scenario, how her patient felt in the scenario, and what they'd want to change in order to feel better in that same scenario at a future point. Such portraits were completed periodically throughout treatment as a way of assessing how the patient was progressing.

That morning, I felt compelled to do a self-portrait and decided that I'd focus on intimacy as a theme.

I turned off my phone to eliminate any distractions, took out my sketchpad, and started to draw my own body. I started by sketching my torso in the nude, positioned slightly sideways. Once I was pleased with how that looked, I drew my legs and then took a step back—something was wrong. I had drawn my toned body accurately, but it wasn't right—it was too revealing. I believed that true sensuality was leaving something to the imagination, so I drew in some black thigh-high stockings and a matching high-cut pair of panties, but left my perky B-cups exposed.

That was better, but something was still missing. I took a deep breath and sketched a figure behind me. I started by making him nude but kept his uniquely male parts hidden behind my body as if they were resting just between the line that separates my cheeks. I took another step back and thought that it was odd that he was naked and I wasn't, so I drew a pair of jeans on him—unbuttoned to add to the sensuality of the picture.

I then drew his arms so that one was resting at his hip and the other was positioned near my stomach. I then drew an arm for myself, resting my hand above the one I'd drawn for his on my stomach—the way I held it suggested I was pushing it towards that delicate spot between my legs. I drew another arm on myself, grabbing the hand of his I'd drawn by his hip.

Once I was happy with the bodies, it was time to draw the faces. I wanted to show an expression of longing on my face and drew it with my eyes closed. I decided to sketch my lips slightly apart to enhance the feeling of sensuality. I then turned to drawing the face of the man behind me, but struggled. I didn't know whose face I was going to draw: Terry's or Jack's.

After struggling for a bit, I came up with another idea. Starting from the bottom of the image, where my lace-clad legs began, I started to draw a plume of smoke which rose through the image, up our bodies, and obscured our faces. Was this a sketch of love being extinguished or of passion igniting? If that psychologist were here, she'd have a field day with that.

It begged the question, though, what was going on inside of me? Why now, after fifteen years of marriage, was I feeling pulled towards someone else? First there was the close call in New York—who knows what would have happened if Marley hadn't stepped it. And then there were all those feelings I was having for Jack—I literally felt as if I was being torn in two.

On Sunday, Marley pushed me to think about what it was about Terry that I was unhappy about and I gave her the knee-jerk answer that I felt as if he no longer put me first. As I stared at my self-portrait, though, I questioned whether or not that was really it. Something about it didn't feel right and as I struggled to think about what it was, I thought about Terry more. No, it wasn't that he didn't put me first, it was how much he had changed.

#

The Terry you have seen thus far was a hard-charging Type-A kind of guy, but as I mentioned a few times before he wasn't always that way. I want to paint a picture of what Terry was like when we first met—before I lost him to the law—so you can better understand what I loved about him.

Terry was my Lloyd Dobler, and if you aren't familiar with that name just picture a young John Cusack holding a boombox over his head and blasting "In Your Eyes" to the girl of his dreams. Lloyd Dobler was his character in *Say Anything*, and, like Lloyd, Terry was an underachiever, not wanting anything more from life than to write his heart out—and write he did.

He graduated after my freshman year and this was in the days when we didn't walk around with cell phones and could keep in touch through texting—even email wasn't all that common back then. As a result, he would write me the most beautiful hand-written letters proclaiming how much he loved me and longed for us to be together, how sad he was that we weren't together. He'd compare his love for me to the number of grains of sand on the beach or the number of stars in the sky—perhaps a bit melodramatic, but it made my nineteen-year-old heart melt.

That's why I had such a hard time with Terry's transformation from Lloyd Dobler into my father—because I knew what he once was and I missed him. To really paint a picture of the Terry that was, I'm going to tell you about the first time we made love as there's no better way to showcase exactly who I fell in love with.

Terry wasn't like other guys I met on campus in that he wasn't a skirt chaser. Sure, there was that episode with Susan I told you about earlier, but that was the exception and certainly not the rule when it came to Terry Gardner —plus, she technically came on to him.

A romantic at heart, the Terry I met in the mid 1990s was a writer with a poet's soul—he didn't care about making money or getting to the next level in his career and certainly didn't put too much thought in anything beyond what was going on in the here and now; he was an in-the-moment kind of guy, and the bohemian in me found that incredibly sexy.

The Terry I met noticed everything—when I'd get my hair cut, if I wore a different perfume, or if my body language suggested that I was having a tough day. At those times he would just hold me as tight as he could and make me feel safe in his arms.

We counted anniversaries in months back then and on our third he took me to a restaurant right over the Massachusetts state line. Our college was based in a small Connecticut farming town full of chain restaurants that weren't the kind of place you'd take someone for a special occasion. Being the romantic that he was, Terry wanted someplace upscale to take me that night, so he borrowed his roommate's beat-up Volkswagen Golf along with an ill-fitting sport coat and took me to a place called Crabtree's.

I'd grown up in Manhattan and had been to my fair share of five-star restaurants, but this was new territory for Terry and he felt uncomfortable from the time he entered the place. I think his mouth was as dry as a bone when he approached the maître d' to give his name for the reservation as he couldn't get his words out—he was that nervous.

Once we sat at the table, I remember grabbing his hands because they were shaking, partly because of feeling like a fish out of water and partly in anticipation of what he thought was going to happen later on. We had talked about taking our relationship to the next step physically— up until then we did everything but have sex—and we both felt that love was in the air that night. He was nervous with anticipation and I thought that was the cutest thing I'd ever seen, a guy nervous about sex.

I'll never forget how he looked at me during dinner. His penetrating hazel eyes felt like they were staring right into my soul—it felt like he never broke eye contact. And that smile! Terry didn't have a wide, full-mouth smile like many guys, his was more like a smirk—a devilish grin that invited danger and excitement concurrently. Between his eyes and his lips, he had me, and I found that my pulse was starting to rise during dinner. Anticipation was building and, later that evening, I hoped it would end in a passionate climax.

Our waiter could tell that we were two young kids in love and treated us to a dessert on him—chocolate-covered strawberries. When they came to the table, Terry, accompanied by his trademark smirk, told me to close my eyes. Even though I felt silly doing so in a restaurant filled with people, I complied.

"Now open your mouth," he said. Again, I did as he asked—it felt so exciting being told what to do.

I felt the tip of the strawberry on my lips and it was electrifying. There was something about the sensory deprivation resulting from my eyes being closed that enhanced this experience. I wanted more of it.

"Don't bite it," he said and pushed it through my lips and into my mouth. I let my tongue caress the sweet flavor of the berry for a minute before taking it all into my mouth.

"Now bite it," he said.

My teeth sank into the strawberry's flesh and a burst of flavor shot straight into my mouth. He repeated this ritual until the bowl was empty.

I can't imagine what the other people in the restaurant

were thinking as they saw this, but what I loved about Terry was that he didn't care, and as a result, I didn't either.

Everything was a blur after that—I don't even remember him paying for the check. What I do remember, vividly, was our holding hands the entire drive back to school and his drawing little hearts on mine with the tip of his finger. He was driving me crazy and I couldn't wait to be alone with him.

We stayed in my room that night because my roommate went home for the weekend. Once we got inside, you'd have thought we'd go at it like two dogs in heat, but Terry was apprehensive—I could tell he was nervous and wanted everything to be just right. At one point, I thought he was actually shivering—he later told me that sexual anticipation did that to him, made his body shiver.

It was a marathon, not a sprint, and he started with a kiss—a deep, open-mouthed kiss so passionate that I felt him breathing into me and I into him. As our tongues met, my body started to long for his and it was me, not him, who made the first move. While maintaining our locked lips, I slid one hand down the front of his body and untucked his shirt. A simple movement, but it had the desired effect as he responded in kind by untucking mine. Then his hand went farther south.

As I felt his fingers between my legs I let out a little gasp and whispered into his ear, "Yes." Just that one word. It was all he needed—before I knew it, I was on my back and he was hovering on top of me.

He broke contact with my mouth and started nibbling on my neck, kissing my chin on the way. I wanted to be free from my clothes, but what he was doing felt so good I simply didn't want to break contact. After a while, he made a trail of kisses from my neck to my chest and started unbuttoning my blouse. I remember him fumbling with the front hook of my bra and my being a bit impatient with his inability to undo it, so I took that as my cue to take charge.

I reached behind his neck and rolled him onto his back. While resting myself on top of him, I unsnapped my bra, removed the straps from my shoulders, and let it fall to the floor.

He had seen me nude before, but this time was different. As his hands reached up to caress my breasts, there was no mistake that he was getting turned as I felt his arousal bulging through his jeans. I leaned in to kiss him on the mouth and reached between my own legs to unbutton his pants, only leaving his lips to tug them off of him. While I freed him from his denim, he sat up and removed his shirt and then, just like I had done to him moments earlier, he turned me onto my back—then the body kissing started.

Terry wasn't in a rush and whispered as much into my ear. He then took his time kissing each of my breasts until my nipples responded with an erection of their own—two can play at this game. He then kissed below my chest, down to my belly button, and rested his mouth on my mound, which was still protected by my tights.

I was self-conscious at first knowing he could feel my excitement seeping through my tights, but this seemed to turn him on even more; he opened his mouth and exhaled onto me—a sensation that drove me wild—his hot breath enveloping the heart of my femininity.

I raised my hips, signaling it was okay to remove my

tights, and he responded by tugging them southward until I was as bare as he was. Then his head went down farther but bypassed my flower—he was such a tease. Instead he kissed my inner thighs and just grazed my opening with the very tip of his tongue. When I couldn't take it any longer I parted my legs and pushed myself forward—the feeling of his tongue on my pearl was electric and I almost climaxed by all he was doing with his mouth, but I longed to feel him inside me and pulled myself back. Everything felt right. I was ready and I wanted to climax with his excitement buried between my legs.

"I want you inside me," I whispered into his ear.

Terry stopped what he was doing and kissed my body on his way back to my face. As he moved upward, I felt his arousal on my sex and decided to guide it in with my hand, but he stopped me.

I thought he was going to ask me to take him into my mouth as I had done a few times in the past, but that wasn't it. He got up, walked over to his pants, and pulled something out of them. A condom.

"I brought this with me."

I took it from him, opened it, and placed the ring on the top of his arousal and slid the sheath down slowly until it was at his base. He resumed the position he was in before and I felt his tip pressing against me. He looked at me in the eyes and smiled. I nodded, signifying it was time. I reached my hand between his legs to guide him inside.

He heard me gasp a bit as his tip entered and rushed himself out quickly.

"Are you okay?"

"Yes," I reassured him. "It's been a while, you have to ease in."

He didn't mind taking it slow and rubbed his head on my pearl before trying to enter again. This time it was easier and he pushed slowly until my muscles relaxed and I welcomed him in. Welcome home, Terry.

This was not one of those kinky sessions where we tried multiple positions or where we glistened in layers of sweat afterwards—those would come later (though they'd never be as rough as I really wanted). That night, slow and steady won the race.

We never broke eye contact and we breathed as if we were one person. As our mutual arousal built, the speed at which he moved on top of me increased and I could feel myself approaching a climax. He reached down between my legs and massaged my pearl while slowly sliding in and out of me until I shuddered underneath him, signaling I had climaxed—he was polite that way, always was, making sure I came first.

"Your turn," I said and then turned him around so that he was on his back. Sitting astride his lap, I reached behind me to guide him back inside and moved my hips up and down until I felt his body tense up and his arousal start to convulse inside me. I felt every pulse of it, every beat. When his climax was done, I rested my hands on his chest, played with his hair, and drifted off to sleep feeling as if everything was right in the world.

I remember waking up a short while later to an empty bed. At first I thought he'd left, but was pleased to find him sitting at my desk writing in his journal. He never shared with me his entry that evening and I'd still love to know what he wrote.

#

I wasn't just upset with Terry for his chosen career path or because he worked long hours—I simply missed who he was back then.

I missed the hopeless, starry-eyed romantic in him—the guy who would write me love letters and who could never wait to see me. In his place, I had this ambitious, driven man who took care of me financially but not emotionally. In turn, I found that the emotional void in my life was longing to be filled, and it was that which was pulling me towards extramarital attention.

CHAPTER FIFTEEN

Wrong Number

I want to be honest about something, a year after this all happened, I still don't know whether to laugh or cry about what Terry did that Wednesday night. I'm biased though, you be the judge. Oh, my snarky asides are back—you'll see why.

#

I'm not a heavy drinker, so to have had multiple shots of Jägermeister throughout the afternoon, followed by the beers I chased them with, left me pretty toasted by the time my siblings left around seven o'clock. Pop started looking a little tired and went to his room, leaving me alone with his buddy Sol.

"Terry," he said to me while I was contemplating going to bed to sleep off the intoxication that had set in. "Can I have a word with you?"

"Fine," I said.

"Let's grab a drink at the bar."

Drink? I'd reached my limit and then some. I walked with him to the Yasgur's Farm South bar, aptly named

Gerry's Place after Pop (or maybe the late Gerry Garcia of Grateful Dead fame) and intended to order a water.

"Two glasses of chardonnay please," Sol said.

Wine? On top of the Jäger and beer, this was certainly going to lead to my early departure from this world.

"You should know that even if he doesn't say it, your father is very proud of you."

These words from Sol sounded sincere, and sitting this close to him I noticed something I hadn't seen before—a gold symbol he wore around his neck. "What is that?" I asked, pointing at it.

"Ah, you little goy, this is my Chai necklace. It is a combination of two Hebrew letters; Chet and Yod. The word Chai means *living* in Hebrew and my daughter bought this necklace for me after I got this." Sol pointed to a scar he had on his thigh. "This is my zipper. It runs from down here all the way up my chest."

"Zipper?"

"Twenty years ago I had a triple bypass. I went to get a life insurance policy and failed a stress test. A day later, I was under the knife—three of my arteries were seventy-five percent clogged. I was a ticking time bomb and could have gone at any minute. She bought this for me as a reminder of the importance of life, a gift from the living God."

"Shit," I said.

"As much as I missed my dear Sharon, who died of cancer five years before my surgery, I wasn't yet ready to see her."

"I'm sorry to…"

Sol waved his hands in front of my face suggesting he didn't want to talk about it. "I didn't call you over here to go on and on about me," he said. "Your father is a close friend to me and I love him like a brother, which means you are practically my little goy nephew. Now this business of you going one hundred and two days without the physical company of your wife has me very concerned."

Holy shit, that's what this was about? I thought he was going to give me some clue as to why Pop was acting so funny. Instead he wants to probe into my love life. I wondered if he was related to Robbie.

"Pop says you are a teacher here," I said, attempting to change the subject. "What are you into? Yoga? Pilates? Tai chi?"

Sol looked to be in as good of shape as any septuagenarian I had ever met, I assumed he was a fitness instructor of some sort. He smiled widely.

"Nice try at attempting to change the subject, but you will find that trying to do so is futile because what I teach will be important to you and your lack of love life. I teach tantra," he said while raising his eyebrows, the way dirty old men do when recalling their honeymoon to someone from a younger generation. The expression on my face gave away my ignorance, so he explained.

"Tantra is not well understood here in the west, but it is the key to healthy living, something that can help transform you into the person that you were meant to be."

For a period of time that afternoon, I'd forgotten that I was at a place called Yasgur's Farm South—my conversation with Sol brought me right back to reality.

"And how does that work?" I asked, taking a sip of the wine I promised myself I wouldn't touch.

With a straight face Sol said, "By not rejecting our bodies and their desires, but embracing them." And then he added, "How often do you masturbate?"

His question caught me off guard and I snarfed up the chardonnay—at least that sip wouldn't contribute to tomorrow's inevitable hangover. "Excuse me?"

"How often do you take yourself out on a date, tickle the pickle, spank the monkey?"

"I know what masturbate means, but why do you want to know?"

"The first step to living a tantric life is to be in touch with yourself, and that means touching yourself… frequently."

"Given my sex life, it's pretty much daily," I admitted. The alcohol I'd been consuming helped to break down my inhibitions and spill the beans to Sol.

"What did you do to cut yourself off from your wife's young yoni? The longest my Sharon withheld was two days."

Two days? Even in the early days of our marriage, we didn't have sex that frequently. What the hell had I been doing wrong?

"She's got issues," was all I could reply.

I was unprepared for the smack he laid on my forehead.

"Hey!" I protested.

"Why are you blaming her? If she's not schtupping you, have you ever thought it just might be your fault?"

My fault? Who does this guy think he is? I have a great job, keep myself in great shape, and am always making suggestive comments that I'd like to have more sex. Whatever is causing her to be frigid is on her, not me. I say as much to Sol.

"You're a putz."

"Excuse me?"

"Listen, Terry, you don't know what you don't know and I'm telling you right now, you don't know a thing about what your wife wants."

"And what does she want, Sol? Enlighten me."

"Do you make her feel as if she is the number one priority in your life?"

"I work long hours and…"

"That's a no then," he said without giving me time to finish.

"Do you have an equal division of labor with all the household chores?"

"Well, she does most of them, but I…"

"Another no." This guy was impatient.

"When was the last time you just grabbed her in the kitchen and told her what you wanted to do to her?"

I've always been a gentle lover to my wife; I'd never dreamed of being that forceful and said as much to Sol.

"That may be just what she is looking for. Ever think of that? Some women just want a man to take charge and be a little alpha."

"Well, no. But it's not like I can do anything about any of those things a few thousand miles away."

Sol looked at me in the eyes and smiled. "What if there was?"

The look of confusion on my face must have suggested I had no idea what he was speaking about, which, of course, I didn't.

"Let me tell you something I heard today," Sol said and then raised his empty glass so the bartender could see it. "Stan, another round for me and my sexually ignorant goyish friend."

"Coming right up," Stan the bartender said.

"I'm a liberal Jew, so I don't pay attention to much of anything the Orthodox have to say, but given my profession, I have taken to listening to a podcast called *The Joy of Text* hosted by an Orthodox rabbi. Today he suggested that sexting one's spouse could actually be a good way to build some sense of anticipation and excitement even before the couple moves to the bedroom. So here's what I'm advising you, my young goyim. Send your wife a dick pic."

Did I just hear that right? Did this seventy-plus-year-old man just advise me to sext my wife? That must have been the alcohol talking, I definitely heard wrong.

"Run that by me again," I said.

"Go back to your room tonight, take out your shvantz, and snap a picture of it. Send it off to your wife with the following note, 'The next time I see you, this is yours.'" *I still can't believe he tried this.*

"Wait, you are actually suggesting that I send my wife a dick pic?" I needed to confirm it.

"Now listen, don't show the whole thing. Just tug down your pants a bit and show her the shaft. And take the picture in black and white, that's more sexy."

Mother of God, was I really having a serious conversation about how to take a good dick pic with a seventy-plus Jewish guy at a commune for aging hippies?

"And if you are lucky, she'll send you a picture of her knish. Now what are you wasting time with me for? Get the hell out of here and be the Annie Leibovitz of your schlong."

He literally pushed me out of my chair and I stumbled my way into the lobby, where I caught the eye of an elderly woman at the front desk.

"You look just like Gerry. He told me his son was going to be staying with us tonight, but he didn't mention how handsome he was." She rubbed up and down my arm as she said this. "Do you want any company tonight?"

Even though I hadn't had sex with another human being in one hundred and two days, I wasn't desperate enough to hook with a seventyish woman who looked like a cross between Rue McClanahan and Joy Behar. I lifted up my left hand and showed her my wedding ring.

"That's a shame, darlin', but let me know if you want a wakeup call," she said while putting her fist to her mouth and simulating oral sex.

"I'll be fine," I said and then took the key from her and walked to my room. *Good call.*

Perhaps it was the alcohol or maybe my own curiosity as to what my wife would say about my sending her a picture of my dick, or a combination of both, but I yanked my briefs down a bit so that my shaft was exposed but the head was tucked underneath the waistband of my briefs. Would a woman think this is hot? *Not this one, idiot.*

I got cold feet and decided to get up and evaluate myself in front of the bathroom mirror. At forty-one, I still looked pretty good. While I'd gone gray around the temples, I'm told that this makes me look distinguished and therefore appealing to women. I tugged my briefs down all the way to see how I looked in the nude and, not to sound egotistical, but I keep myself in good shape. I eat well, exercise regularly, and still have the six-pack I had back in my college days. What the hell, I said to myself, and went back to my bed to snap the picture—my first ever dick pic.

After I opened my text messaging app to send the pic I

just took to Libby, I realized I never got back to Marley about what she wanted to talk to me about the night before. I typed her a note telling her I just got to my room and would reach out to her tomorrow

I then loaded up the picture I had just taken and tapped out the following note to my wife, "The next time I see you, this is yours," and then hit send. Although I didn't send it to my wife. I could blame it on the alcohol or perhaps a Freudian slip, but that message and picture of my shvantz, as Sol called it, went right to my wife's best friend Marley. *Oops.*

"Fuck!" I shouted out in my hotel room and then tapped frantically on the phone to try and undo what I did, but the word "delivered" came across my screen. Just as I started typing an apology, I saw three little dots come across the screen signaling that Marley was responding. I typed feverishly to get my note to her, but she'd beaten me to it. I was surprised to see a smiley emoticon. *This is still painful for me.*

Three dots again, followed by a reply which I assumed would be a chastisement but instead felt more like an invitation.

M: It's about time you came to your senses, Terry.

I was at a loss for words, but apparently Marley wasn't.

T: That was meant for Libby.

M: It's mine now. What are you going to do with that?

T: Look, Marley I can explain.

M: Shut up Terry and show me the head.

Holy shit did she want to see more of it? What the hell was happening? Whatever it was, it was incredibly wrong, yet I felt exhilarated.

M: I'm waiting.

Christ, she was impatient. Libby always said she was the dominant type, but I never knew what she meant by that.

M: The head, or I send what you just sent me to Libby.

Fuck, what was I going to do? I tugged my briefs all the way down, rubbed myself a bit to get the blood flowing, snapped another picture and sent it over. I started to shiver at what was going on.

M: That's exactly how I remember it in art class twenty years ago. It would be a shame if Libby found out about this.

She couldn't attempt to blackmail me twice over the same thing, could she? Perhaps Dominants didn't abide by the same set of rules as us vanilla types. Anyways, wouldn't admitting to this compromise her relationship with my wife? And what could possibly be in it for her?

M: You have some hard lessons to learn, Terry Gardner, and I'm going to teach them to you. From now on I am Goddess Marley to you. Do you understand?

T: Yes.

M: Yes what?

What the fuck was she looking for?

M: Yes Goddess, Terry. Say yes Goddess!

Christ, she was tough.

T: Yes, Goddess.

M: That's a good boy. Now when you come to the art exhibition tomorrow night, and you will come Terry, you and I are going to have a little talk and then start our lessons afterwards. Do you understand?

T: Yes, Goddess.

M: Quick learner.

After that, our exchange was over. I thought to myself, what the hell had I gotten into? *A steaming pile of shit.*

CHAPTER SIXTEEN

Lloyd Dobler Returns

It's still painful to revisit that exchange, but I've learned that what happened that night happened for a reason— although it took me some time to figure out what that reason actually was.

While Terry was partying with his siblings and later taking some ill-conceived advice from his new BFF Sol, I was working like a madwoman transforming the sketch I worked on earlier into a full-fledged painting.

It normally takes me a good twenty hours to take a sketch I've made and bring it to life on a canvas, but Wednesday afternoon and into the very wee hours of Thursday morning, I worked like a woman possessed. I worked as fast and furiously as Bob Ross; that is, if Bob Ross painted erotic scenes instead of natural landscapes.

At two in the morning I took a step back and allowed myself a smile at what I'd created. It was beautiful and certainly fit in the *Love on the Rocks* theme I conceived for the show.

Since nothing of interest happened to me before my

exhibition later that day, I'm going to finish sharing with you what happened to Terry on his last day in Florida.

#

I woke up with all the telltale signs of a hangover: headache, dry mouth, and, of course, regret. Did I really send a picture of my, what did Sol call it, shvantz, to my wife's best friend? Did she really ask to see more of it? While I was lying in bed and pondering what I had gotten myself into, my phone vibrated and I prayed it wasn't Marley looking for sexting, round two. It wasn't.

It was an email from Paul Hewson's administrative assistant, Mrs. Robinson, informing me that our plans for the day had changed. We were no longer to meet at Paul's golf course, I was now supposed to report to the office ASAP.

I looked outside to see if the weather could explain the change of venue, but it was a beautiful day in South Florida.

"Shit!" I screamed out loud and assumed it had to have something to do with my name showing up in the newspaper.

I showered, got dressed, and then remembered I didn't have a car and thought I'd have to Uber it to the office. Just as I'd pulled my phone out to arrange for an Uber, I ran in to Pop in the lobby.

"Terry, lad, did you sleep well?"

"Pop, look, I need to get to the office right away."

"I'll give you a lift, no detours this time, I promise. Where's the office?"

"Oakland Park and Bayview," I responded.

"That's only ten minutes from here, fifteen if we get caught at the bridge."

There are a number of bridges that let cars over the Intracoastal Waterway and open twice an hour, stopping the flow of traffic, to let the numerous boats traveling up and down the Intracoastal through—I prayed that we made the bridge as I was anxious about the meeting and wanted no delays. Sure enough, the bridge was going up as we turned onto Oakland Park Boulevard.

"Damnit," I said.

"Relax, son, it's only five minutes."

I replied with a sigh.

"Look, this is actually good timing. There's something I want to talk to you about."

Uh-oh, I thought. This couldn't be good.

"I didn't want to say anything to you kids last night because you were all having such a good time and I was enjoying seeing you all together, but there's something you should know."

"What's the matter, Pop?"

"I started feeling sick a few months back. Pain in my chest, thought it was just a bad cold so I let it go, but it didn't go away."

Although I was impatient for the bridge to go back down and anxious for my meeting, I knew better than to rush Pop's story.

"Shit, there's no easy way to say it, but I've got cancer, Terry. It's pretty bad."

"What?" I asked. "How…"

"Started in the lungs, spread to the brain, my bones, it's everywhere. The chemo has been making me sick and it's only prolonging the inevitable. I told my doctor yesterday that I was stopping treatment."

"But Pop…"

"Now you are the only one who knows. The others all live down here and I will be telling them soon, so don't go spilling the beans on me."

"Maybe we could get a second opinion…"

He cut me off again. "This is it, kiddo."

After he said that, the bridge started to go down, apparently serving as a signal that he could go forward and change the subject at the same time.

"What's this meeting about anyway?"

At the time I was still busy processing all he had just admitted and didn't hear his question.

"What's this meeting about? Why are you so anxious?"

I told Pop about how close I was to making partner and that this meeting was a tie-breaker. I also acknowledged my fear that the sudden change of venue had something to do with our names being in the paper.

"Are you open to a little fatherly advice?"

"Sure, Pop." I was curious as to what advice this aging hippie could possibly give me.

"If they don't give you what you want, tell them to fuck off."

I just looked at him.

"I'm serious. If they don't recognize the contribution you've made to that organization, tell them you will take your talent elsewhere. It will be their loss."

I opened my mouth, but words didn't come out. A moment later, we had crossed the bridge and then pulled into the firm's parking lot.

"That's not how it works, Pop."

"Who are you kidding, of course that's how it works. That's how it always works. They have the power, you are the labor. If they value your labor and you threaten to walk out, they'll give you what you want."

My head was overloaded with information. I didn't want to leave Pop after the news he just told me, but at the same time I really needed to get inside. I assumed that, even if he was as sick as he said he was, I'd still have more time with him.

"I need to go right back to Connecticut tonight because Libby has an art exhibition, so I'll just take a cab back to the airport. I'll get back down soon, Pop."

"No matter what has happened in the past, Terry, please know that I love you. Never forget that the greatest gift you could give someone else is your time. If there's any regret I have in life it's that I didn't spend enough time with you and your siblings. Promise me you won't make the same mistake I did and that you will give freely of your time to those whom you love. If you do that, I will feel as if I succeeded as a father."

"I promise, Pop."

He got out of the car and hugged me goodbye and I had the sad realization that this might be one of the last times I'd see him alive. He held his hug a few beats too long and then got back into his car and popped the trunk so I could get my clubs out. After I watched his car turn left onto Oakland Park Boulevard, I entered the building, and before I knew it Mrs. Robinson was escorting me to Paul Hewson's office.

"He's finishing up a meeting, Mr. Gardner. Just have a seat here and he'll buzz me when he's ready."

As with Tuesday, that Thursday morning Mrs. Robinson was all business. I took a seat in the waiting room outside Paul's office and waited. After about twenty minutes, I'd gone through all of my emails, text messages, and exhausted all social network feeds.

I experienced first hand how quirky Paul was on Tuesday when he took me on a tour of my hometown. I also knew he had a reputation for power moves, and making junior staffers wait was pretty much at the top of all power moves. Without anything left to entertain me, I stared at the ceiling for a minute and then remembered that I packed my old journals in my briefcase and decided to rifle through them.

As I reread my reflections from all those years ago, I realized how much I'd changed since those days. I still loved Libby dearly, but since transitioning into my career as a lawyer I'd stuffed her in the back seat and put my career in the front. As I reflected on this, I started to hate the man I'd become, and the sad thing is, at the time, I thought it's what she wanted.

#

A year after we'd started dating, I was working in publishing and barely made enough money to afford my rent. I worked in Manhattan, where Libby lived with her parents, and vividly remember the Christmas Eve I spent with her family because I couldn't afford to leave New York and spend it with mine down in Florida.

Libby's parents had resigned themselves to the fact that their daughter wasn't just having a fling with me and that I was likely here to stay long term. Sensing this, her father took me aside after the meal while Libby and her mother took care of the dishes. Clichéd, I know, but she came from a very traditional household.

"Terry, I think we should have a talk about your future," her father, Christoph Anderson, said while handing me a glass full of Scotch.

He then added, "Twenty-five-year-old single malt, it's meant to be sipped."

He was always trying to educate me on the rituals of the rich.

"My future?"

"I'm a straight shooter, Terry. I've known Libby a lot longer than you have and she's going through a wild child phase right now, but it will pass. My advice, if you don't want to be just a phase in her life, you need to set your sights on a real career."

"Publishing isn't a real career?"

He looked at me dead in the eyes. "Put simply, no. What do you earn per year?"

"Twenty-three thousand dollars," I replied. Up until that point, I'd never given much thought to money—I was just happy to be working in a field I was passionate about.

"I made that last month, and it was a bad month." *Asshole*.

I hated showoffs.

"I'm not saying this to brag, but to paint a picture of what your life could be like. You are a smart guy, Terry, I see that, and you've got a good look about you. You are well spoken and clearly know how to write and make an argument—you'd make a great lawyer."

I resented that little talk for a while, but the seed he had planted had taken root in my mind and at every gathering he would water it and give it sunlight.

If my Paul Hewson was the Ghost of Christmas Past and my own father was the Ghost of Christmas Present, Christoph Anderson was the Ghost of Christmas Yet to Come—and just like the one in Dickens' story, he painted a bleak picture of my future. The last thing I wanted was to lose the love of my life so, behind her back, I prepared for the LSATs and worked on applications to law school—the rest was history.

My concentration was broken by Mrs. Robinson, who waved her hands trying to get my attention.

#

"Are you awake over there, Mr. Gardner? Mr. Hewson will see you now."

I snapped out of my daydream, grabbed my bag, and walked into Paul Hewson's office, where I was shocked to find all six of the firm's senior partners waiting for me. They were seated in a semicircle with Paul in the middle: three people to his left and three to his right. Paul was wearing his trademark sunglasses, but today he wasn't dressed like an aging rock star, he was in a long silk robe looking as if he'd just auditioned for a part in a Bollywood production.

He motioned for me to take a seat in the middle of the room and I felt as if I was about to be interrogated; the thought of Paul's glaucoma and the setting of the room reminded me of the fact that I had been cited for possession of marijuana that I technically didn't even possess.

As I looked at the scowl on Preston's face, I remembered what he said at the golf course on Sunday—if I got caught with pot, my employment would be terminated. That's it, they read the paper. My goose was cooked.

"Mr. Gardner, sorry for the change of venue, but given what we have to tell you it was important to do it in the office." Paul's brogue sounded more menacing today than it did on Tuesday, as if he was doing his best Liam Neeson impersonation and I assumed the phrase "I have a specific set of skills" was about to come out of his mouth. Fuck!

I scanned the room to see if anyone's expression betrayed why they were there, but their poker faces were in full swing. Even Cassidy Clarke, who was typically jovial, was all business.

"You started at this firm in July of 2002 and ever since then, you've been an eagle employee. You've billed more hours than anyone in your flight and for that you should be commended."

Note, in any other firm I'd be part of the class of 2002, but my firm's infatuation with golf divided us into flights.

"You have shown dedication and devotion to the firm of Hewson, Evans, Mullen, and Clayton and, as you know, not all associates become partners, that's just the way it is. We only admit the best of the best into the rank of partner."

I had the feeling he was building me up for disappointment—that what happened with Pop at the pier Monday night was about to come back and bite me in the ass.

"But even the best of the best are not good enough. Sometimes the best of the best have a fall from grace. Look at Tiger Woods and you'll know what I mean."

Here it comes, my termination notice.

"But fortunately, you've managed to keep squeaky clean during your time here and I understand that you are interested in spearheading our legal cannabis practice, and by what I hear from my peers in California and Colorado, there's a lot of money in that field."

Holy shit, I thought to myself, I think he's going to name me a partner. This game of ping-pong I was playing in my mind was making me dizzy.

"I know that the senior partners are divided on whether or not to promote you, so they punted the decision down to me. After going through your file and listening to my team, and spending the day with you on Tuesday, I've made the decision to name you the next partner of Hewson, Evans, Mullen, and Clayton."

All seven of them started clapping, yet I was instantly put into a daze. My firm's eccentric founder just gave me the news I'd been chasing for the past fifteen years and now, deep down inside me, I questioned whether or not I wanted it.

I thought about the entry in my diary that I wrote the night Libby and I first made love and how far I'd come from the idealistic young man who wrote that. I thought about how my ambition drove a wedge between me and Libby and how upset she was at my coming down to Florida and potentially missing her exhibition. I thought about how much she resented her father and how much like her father I'd become.

I then thought of Pop and the promise I made to him right before we hugged goodbye. Could I give all of my loved ones a generous amount of my time if I made the leap to partner? I remembered Paul being on call after call as we drove to and from Plantation on Tuesday. I then thought, if I were working eighty-hour weeks now, what would I have to work when I had a team of people under me? I'd not only be responsible for doing my own work but overseeing the work and development of others.

"I can tell you're speechless, Terry, but show some sign that you heard what I just said." Paul's six apostles all laughed when he said this.

I then remembered what my father told me in the car before we arrived at the office, *If they don't give you what you want, tell them to fuck off.*

The thing is, the founder of my firm just gave me what I thought I wanted, but I didn't feel right. A lightbulb went off in my head.

"Mr. Hewson, I'm flattered by your kind words, but I can't accept your offer at this time."

I looked around the room and saw the blood drain from everyone's faces—in the history of the firm, no one had ever turned down a partnership.

"Explain," Paul said quizzically. He wasn't angry, simply curious.

"I'd love to," I replied while getting up, "but I am going to be late for an art show." He offered me the faintest of smiles as I rose to leave.

I left all of the senior partners of the firm stunned as I exited the room, dancing like George Banks after he told the managers of the Dawes, Tomes, Mousely, Grubbs Fidelity Fiduciary Bank to practically fuck off. I had a marriage to save and I wasn't going to let anything get in my way.

CHAPTER SEVENTEEN

Alone Again

Had I known what happened in Florida—that Terry walked out on his partnership after coming to the realization that he did not like who he became—things may have been different. Of course, though, I only learned about all of that well after the fact and, unlike good old Marty McFly, I don't have access to a time-traveling DeLorean. Put simply, there's nothing I can do to change what happened the night of my exhibition.

I now know that when I was getting ready at home for my art show, Terry was trying desperately to get an early flight back to New York but that all flights were booked and he had to settle for waiting in the standby queue for a later afternoon option.

At the time, though, I hadn't heard a word from him except for the voicemail he left me while I was lost when painting my most recent work. Later I'd come to learn that he didn't call me and tell me he turned down the partnership because he was trying to surprise me and have his own Lloyd-Dobler-boombox-over-the-head moment outside of my gallery in Westport. Of course, it didn't work out that way.

No, at the time I was Libby Gardner who believed her marriage was on the rocks, that her husband didn't truly love her, and who had a serious case of wanting-to-jump-her-trainer's-bones disease. Unfortunately, to that last point, I have to admit that Jack Gregory, The Rock of Westport, looked really fucking good that night.

I know what I did that night was wrong and am fond of saying I've been disappointing people since 1978, but I've teased this night long enough and now it's time that I share what exactly happened during and after my exhibition.

The show started at seven p.m. and featured fifteen paintings from my entire career that showed couples at the end of their relationship; it wouldn't take a Freudian analyst to surmise this theme was a reflection of how I was feeling at the time—that my own marriage was coming to an end.

The first half hour of the show consisted of passed hors d'oeuvres and an open bar. At 7:30 I gave a brief introduction to the evening and explained the theme and then introduced a speaker from the charity I was raising money for as a way of reminding everyone where their money was going. With that behind me, I walked the floor and answered questions about my work as they came up. Interestingly, the most questions I got concerned the painting I had finished very early that morning—it actually went through a bidding war. The subject of the painting seemed relatable to many who attended.

Marley frequently checked in on me to make sure I had everything I needed and, bless her heart, to make sure my wine glass was at least half full every time she saw me. However, I found myself avoiding anything more than superficial contact with her—something still bothered me about how she spoke of my husband both the other night at the comedy club and at the Duck the prior Sunday.

Throughout the evening, I found myself looking at the door frequently and I wish I could say it was to try and spot my husband walk in, but I have to be truthful with you (it's a PET rule after all), I was really on the lookout for Jack and was eager to see him make his entrance, which he did at quarter past eight.

When Jack walked through the door it was as if time stood still and everyone around me ceased to be there. For that moment, it was just him and me. In my mind's eye, I thought back to the fantasy I had while he stretched me out earlier in the week—that's when the butterflies started to flutter in the center of my body. As my eyes drank his muscular form in, those butterflies migrated south, where they fluttered between my legs.

He was certainly dressed to impress; I was used to seeing him in workout clothes, but that night he put on a form-fitting suit that showed off his strong physique—it was almost as if it had been custom tailored for him. His hair was combed perfectly, parted from left to right. Gone was the five o'clock shadow—tonight he was clean shaven and looked more like one of Westport's young hedge fund millionaires than the guy who trains their wives. Capping off his look was a pocket square that matched his pink tie perfectly—he was a man who certainly didn't cut corners when it came to fashion. Our eyes met and locked for a minute. I offered him a slight smile and then waved him over.

"Thank you so much for coming," I said and offered him a hug. He replied by kissing me on the cheek. The scent of his aftershave lingered for a moment after he pulled his face back; the combination of the heat coming off his lips as they touched my cheek and the scent of his cologne made those butterflies between my legs flutter even faster. I knew then and there that I had to have him; tonight was going to be the night.

This was a night that I'd been planning for months, but now I couldn't wait for it to be over. By all accounts, it was a successful evening—not only did I receive many compliments on my work from anyone who's anyone in Westport, but between my paintings and a number of other silent auction items, we'd managed to raise mid five figures for kids with cancer.

I, of course, stayed until all my guests left and then spent some time getting things back in order as I was going to be open for business the following morning. Marley and Jack helped out and by 10 p.m. I was ready to close up shop.

It wasn't lost on me that Terry hadn't shown up or even called, and that fueled in me the desire for revenge—he knew how important this night was for me and he promised me he'd be there. That he didn't make an effort to show said it all, or so I thought at the time.

"You need anything else?" Marley asked as we walked to the door.

Yes, Marley. I need you to stop thinking about my husband's penis and then I need Jack Gregory to take me from behind and have his way with me. Of course I think it but don't say it.

"I think I'm good. Going to call it a night," I said.

I locked up the gallery and then walked with both of them to the parking lot but stumbled a bit on the way to my car.

"How much did you have to drink?" Jack asked.

"I lost count after four," I replied.

"I can't let you drive home, you are one of my best clients and I can't afford the income hit if you wrapped yourself around a tree and weren't able to train."

"Let's walk back to my place and I'll give you a ride," Marley said. She lived in walking distance to my gallery in an apartment over one of Main Street's restaurants.

"It's no problem for me to give her a ride," Jack replied.

"Thanks, Jack, you can consider this repayment for canceling on me this morning."

Marley wore a worried look on her face as I got into Jack's car, though I really didn't care what she thought— she who clearly fantasized over my husband.

During the entire ride home from the gallery, all I thought about was how I was going to get Jack into my bed, which of course was risky given I had no idea when Terry was coming home. Given that he didn't show up at my exhibition or even bother to call, I assumed he was staying down in Florida at least one more day and thought I was safe.

Jack pulled into the driveway and I could see that Terry still wasn't home. I needed to get Jack inside the house and the only thing I could think of to say was, "I know this may sound silly, but would you mind walking me to the door? There was a burglary in the neighborhood not too long ago and I don't feel comfortable walking there by myself."

Jack looked at me, smiled, and said, "Of course." He

even got out of the car and walked around to my side and opened the door for me, thereby stoking the fire he set ablaze when he kissed me hello back at the gallery.

As we walked towards the front door, I combed through my purse for my keys. I opened the door but turned around and saw that Jack was hesitant to come inside.

"Stay with me for a drink," I said. "I'm so keyed up about how well tonight went, I don't want the night to end just yet."

He looked hesitant. Was it not obvious what my intentions were?

"Come on, live a little, Mr. Rock of Westport."

Jack acquiesced, "One drink, that's it. I have an early session tomorrow."

I showed him to the living room and then walked into the kitchen and poured two glasses of Scotch; while I hated my father, I inherited his appreciation for the stuff.

"So what was this emergency you had this morning?" I called from the kitchen.

"A client of mine wasn't feeling well after an early workout," he said. "I went with her to the hospital to make sure she was okay and felt as if I should stay until her son got there."

Oh my goodness, life was starting to imitate my dreams. How I hoped the rest of my dream from the other day would come true—just the thought of it made me flush with excitement.

I sat next to Jack on the couch and just looked over his body for a moment. He was so strong and I got lost daydreaming about what it would be like for him to hold me, pin me down, and make me his—his strong arms and hands making me feel safe and protected while at the same time he took what he wanted from my body.

In that moment I went through the entire scene I had constructed in my mind—his leaving no square inch of my body un-kissed, the eye contact we would maintain while he took me into his mouth and made love to me with his tongue. How I would caress his excitement and tease him before allowing him to slip inside me. How he would hold my hands as he thrusted in and out of me, taking me to the edge of paradise. And, of course, how we would come together over and over again throughout the course of the night.

I had been fantasizing about him for so long, I knew that it was now or never, so I surprised him by getting up from where I was sitting and straddled him on the couch.

"Libby," he said, but I put a finger to his lips signaling that he shouldn't talk. I replaced that finger with my lips and opened my mouth to his, inviting his tongue inside. As our tongues touched, a feeling of electricity surged through my body and I started losing control, grinding on him like a woman who's completely lost control of herself.

I grabbed his hands and placed them on my backside and hiked the dress I was wearing up so that his long fingers grasped both of my bare cheeks. I then slid my right hand between my legs and rested it on his lap—I could tell he had great control as he wasn't even hard yet. In my mind his superior control meant that this was going to be a good night.

After a moment of going at it hard, I sensed that something was the matter and paused; Jack looked like a deer in headlights. "What's the matter?" I asked.

"Libby, I think you have the wrong idea about me."

Wrong idea? Yes, I had all the wrong ideas about him—

my entire fantasy life for the past few months was based solely on all the wrong ideas about Jack Gregory—The Rock of Westport. But, speaking of rocks, I realized something at that moment; Jack's entire body was rock hard except for one part—the part I had been massaging in my hands for a few moments. The kissing, grinding, and touching hadn't made it move at all, and then it hit me like a splash of cold water to my face. I figured out what Jack meant when he said I had the wrong idea about him.

"Libby, I'm gay."

Gay! It figures that at my second at bat in the cheating game I swing and miss yet again. I don't even bother getting up and just bury my head inside his neck and start crying. He pats me on the back as an attempt to console the wailing woman on his lap.

With Jack pinned under me and me sobbing as loudly as I was, I didn't even hear the car pull up in the driveway, nor did I hear that same car's door open and close. It goes without saying that I didn't hear the garage door open or my husband enter our house from the mudroom adjacent to the garage. Needless to say, I was crying so loudly that the first time I heard my husband that night was after he had entered the living room and saw me sitting astride my trainer when he simply said, "Libby, what the fuck?"

Before I even had a chance to reply, Terry had hightailed it out of our home. I heard his car door slam and then the sound of screeching tires heading for God knows where. Jack followed suit shortly after and just like that I was all alone again in my home, chock-full of regret and left wondering how the fuck I was going to recover from this.

My first instinct was to get into my car and drive around town searching for Terry, but then I realized that I'd left it at the gallery. I couldn't exactly hail an Uber because I'd feel like a complete idiot telling the driver to just drive around Westport until we found my husband's Porsche.

I tried his cell phone, but he didn't pick up. I thought about calling Marley, but I knew that she was just going to lay the I-told-you-so trip on me. So, instead of taking any action whatsoever, that night I threw a pity party and cried myself to sleep.

CHAPTER EIGHTEEN

The Mentor

I said that I cried myself to sleep that night, but the truth is I didn't sleep at all. At the time I was experiencing a roller coaster of emotions: anger at Terry for missing my exhibition, humiliation at throwing myself at my gay trainer, and fear that my marriage was soon to be over.

As you will see, though, I wasn't the only person who had trouble sleeping that night—Terry faced his own struggles. No snarky comments from me on Terry's reflection of what he did after he left the house because, given what I'd done, I didn't have a right to say anything.

#

I was pretty keyed up on the ride from the airport to my wife's gallery. Earlier in the day, I'd turned down the partnership I'd been chasing for fifteen years all because I realized how much of a jerk I'd been to my wife ever since I started practicing law. I rushed to the airport only to find all flights from Fort Lauderdale to New York were booked —Pop was right, damn snowbirds!

As my name wasn't called on the standby list for any of

the early afternoon flights, I started to get nervous but was fortunate to get a seat on the four p.m. flight to White Plains, which would get me in at seven p.m., though high winds in Westchester led to our circling over Long Island Sound and my plane didn't land until 8:30.

I took a cab from the airport to my office so that I could pick up my car, but construction on Connecticut's Merritt Parkway had me in bumper-to-bumper traffic all the way back to Westport. By the time I had my wheels, I didn't make it to Libby's gallery until 10:30—by then her exhibition was over and she'd gone back home.

As I drove home, I rehearsed in my mind what I would say to her and asked myself, *what would Lloyd Dobler do?* I did not have a boombox and my Peter Gabriel tapes were long gone, but what I did have were my journals and I planned on storming into the house and reading some excerpts from the time we first met as a peace offering.

I got home to find a strange car in my driveway—when I saw Libby straddling some muscle-bound jock on the couch, my heart practically stopped beating. My fight-or-flight response kicked in and I chose the latter. Before you judge me, I'll point out that the woman of my dreams was in the arms of a much larger man, and I'm not what you call a fighter.

After I got in my car I realized I had no place to go; I had no family in the Northeast and the prospect of staying in a hotel alone after awakening my inner Lloyd Dobler was beyond depressing. I thought about calling my friend Robbie, but that would lead to a conversation I wasn't interested in having at the time. That's when I remembered the text exchange I'd had with Marley the night before. What was it she said, "You and I are going to have a little talk and then start our lessons." What did she mean by that? I texted her and told her that I needed to speak with her. Marley's reply was instantaneous.

M: What's the matter?

T: I found Libby at home with some Jock.

M: Come over, now!

Marley lives in an apartment above a restaurant on Westport's Main Street. Fortunately, I was able to find parking along the street—there's a small lot in the back for residents and visitors, but Main Street was better lit and I don't like leaving my car anywhere dark overnight.

I walked over to the door to her place and hit the button corresponding to her apartment to announce I was there. A moment later, a buzzer sounded, unlocking the door, so I pulled it open and entered the building.

A quick walk of the stairs later and I was standing in front of her door—she had left it ajar and I pushed it slowly and entered what could best be described as her lair. It was dark, except for the light from a few candles that I could tell were recently lit as the scent of spent sulfur from a match still lingered in the air.

"Where were you tonight, Terry?" Marley's voice startled me. I turned around to see her standing in the hallway, clad in black lace lingerie and holding something in her hand, though I couldn't tell what it was.

"I just found…"

Marley cut me off. "I didn't ask what you just found, Terry, I asked where you were."

As she got closer, I noticed that her long red hair was pulled tightly back and that she was wearing blood-red lipstick. As she came closer, I could see that she was holding a riding crop in her hand—my heart started to race while I explained my travel hiccups.

"Hold out your hands, Terry."

"What?'

"Hold. Out. Your. Hands. Terry." Each word was spoken slowly, with impatience.

"Okay," I said while extending my hands.

"Okay, what?" Marley asked, and I recalled what she asked I call her the night before.

"Okay, Goddess."

Marley offered a slight smile and then whipped my hands with the riding crop. It hurt but was oddly sensual.

"You've been a very bad boy, Terry Gardner. Sending pictures of yourself to your wife's best friend. You must be punished for that. Get on your knees."

Did she just ask me to get on my knees? All I was looking for was a shoulder to cry on and she's getting me involved in an S&M session. When I didn't comply, she raised the crop to accentuate her command, and that motivated me towards compliance.

"Yes, Goddess," I said while going down to the floor.

"Terry, Terry, Terry," she said while walking around me. I was waist level with her and it was hard to take my eyes off of the lower half of her body. Her lacy undergarments were hypnotic, and the blood was rushing from my brain and directly towards my penis.

"Do you like what you see, Terry?"

"Yes, Goddess," I said and then reached out to touch her legs. She responded with a slap to my wrist from her riding crop.

"You will not touch me, Terry. You will not even look at me."

To make sure I followed these rules, she produced a

blindfold—from where I don't know—and placed it over my eyes. She then walked around to my back.

"Place your hands behind your back," she commanded.

"Yes, Goddess," I replied and did as I was told.

She then tied them up with some kind of zip tie. Goddamn, this girl was kinky. I had no idea.

"Now tell me what you saw tonight when you went home."

"This morning I…"

She cut me off with a slap to the hands from her riding crop.

"I didn't ask about this morning, I asked about tonight."

"Sorry, Goddess," I responded and then told her about walking in on Libby and Mr. Muscles.

"That man has been coming to your house three times a week for the past few years and you don't even know his name. Isn't that sad?"

"The past few years? She's been fucking him for that long?"

I received a hard slap across my ass from Marley's riding crop for that outburst.

"She's not fucking him at all. The only guy she has fucked in the past twenty years is you. But tell me, Terry, can you think of any reasons why your wife might be tempted to step out on you?"

The question hung in the air while I reflected on how I'd changed over the years. There's nothing like being blindfolded and on your knees with your hands tied behind your back and the threat of corporal punishment looming over you to get you to start thinking clearly.

I confessed the epiphany I had come to earlier, that I'd

shoved Libby aside to focus on my career and added how intent I was to change that. I told her about turning down the offer to become a partner at my firm and how I wanted nothing more than to be the man I was when Libby and I were first together. To live up to the promise I had made to myself twenty years ago—to put her first, now and always.

"So why did you come here? To revenge fuck her best friend?"

"No, Goddess," I said. "I came here because I have no one else to talk to."

"What about your friend Robbie?" Marley asked.

"I'm sorry, Goddess, but I'm afraid Robbie doesn't exactly provide the world's greatest advice."

It's true, had I gone to Robbie's place, he'd have responded by ordering two escorts for in-call service and left me with the bill. Also, I'm not sure how his mother would have reacted after two women of the evening arrived at her home only to find her son shuffling them downstairs to his basement apartment.

Marley then asked, "Do you think you could forgive your wife for what she did tonight?"

I thought about it. I had a close call in Denver and even though it didn't go as far as Libby and her trainer took it, I was guilty of some breach of the marital contract.

"In time, I think so," I said. "I love her."

"That settles it then," Marley said. I then heard her walk out of the room. A few moments later she was back and I felt her cut off the zip ties that were binding my hands. After that, she removed my blindfold and I could see that she'd changed into sweatpants and a sweatshirt. Her hair that was originally pulled back tightly now fell around her shoulders.

"Thank you, Goddess."

"You can cut the Goddess crap, Terry," she said. "The Dom session is over."

"Last night you said that my education would begin today. What did you mean by that?"

"Terry, you've already come to the realization that you've been acting like an asshole for years, I was simply going to point that out to you, but you beat me to it."

"And the whole dick pic thing, you know that was an accident, right? I meant for that to go to Libby."

"I figured as much. I was just fucking with you."

I was relieved, but still had a problem on my hands. "What the hell am I going to do about my wife's throwing herself into the arms of another man? Maybe you need to have one of these sessions with her?"

I'll admit that I'm a stereotypical guy and the thought of my wife being tied up and blindfolded while her best friend, clad in lace, walked around her and asked questions was a turn-on.

"No," she said. "You have to speak with her. You have to tell her everything you just told me and then ask for her forgiveness."

"I'm not the one who strayed!" I protested.

"You're right, your mistress wasn't a person, but you did have a mistress. You put your wife aside to focus on your career and, in some ways, that's worse than being stepped out on for another woman."

"How do you figure?" I asked.

"Because at least when a woman is involved we can point to her and say, 'It must be because she has something I don't have,' but when it's work we are at a complete loss. Terry, you weren't there for her when she needed you. You all but abandoned her, and that's precisely why you owe her an apology."

"So I just apologize and wait for her to do the same?"

"No," she said.

Now I was getting confused.

"I'm going to tell you something about your wife, Terry, something I've known since we met. She's a submissive. In my hobby I would refer to her as a sub."

"What does that mean?"

"It means that her partner has to be the one to take charge in everything, from initiating interpersonal contact to directing what happens in the bedroom."

"You are kidding, right? My wife has no interest in sex."

"That's where you are wrong, Terry. She and I hold no secrets from each other. Do you know how many times she has told me she wished you would just come up from behind her and dominate her?"

"Really?" I was stunned. I always thought my wife wanted a gentle love life, I never knew that she wanted a little roughness in the boudoir.

"That's because she never told you and that's a direct result of her submissive tendencies, but it's also because you never asked."

"But every time I've tried to speak with her about sex, we've always wound up in an argument."

"Tell me something, Terry, how do you bring it up?"

"What do you mean?"

"Jesus Christ, for a successful lawyer you are really dense. Okay, let's try this another way. Pretend I'm Libby and you want to talk to me about our sex life. What would you say?"

This was getting weird, but I thought, what the hell, why not give it a try?

"How come we never have sex anymore?"

Apparently, the riding crop stayed around even though Marley had shed the Dom outfit she was wearing because she produced it with lightning speed and slapped me in the thigh with it.

"Ow!" I said.

"Think about how you just asked the question, *how come we never have sex anymore?* The way you say it places all the blame squarely on Libby and you accept no responsibility. It's no wonder she cut you off."

"She told you about that?"

"We keep no secrets from each other."

"Well, how should I say it then?"

"Start by telling her what you miss about being with her sexually. I guarantee if you started with, *I miss being one with you, Libby, and long for your body so that I may feel complete, and I'm going to kick-start our sex life* you would get a lot further than asking *why don't we have sex anymore?*

"That's good advice," I admitted.

"I'm a subject matter expert in sex, Terry. I know what I'm talking about, but there's another thing you are going to have to learn in order to re-ignite the passion inside your wife, and there is passion in there, Terry. A lot of it."

She held my interest. "What's that?"

"You have to learn to be dominant. You have always been a respectful and polite lover to Libby, and believe me, she appreciates that, but you are not fulfilling her every need. She's a total sub, and you have some sub tendencies, too, from what she's told me, but I can tell that you are a switch."

I'm brought back to the land of confusion with all this terminology. "What is a switch?"

"A switch is someone who can flow between being submissive and being dominant depending on the situation."

As Marley spoke, I could tell that she was right. I thought about the fantasy I have about Sue from college and how it felt so good to be submissive with her and let her take control. But I also know that many times I felt the urge to take charge and run the show, it's just that I hold back for fear of upsetting my wife and revealing how freaky I am. I shared all of this with Marley.

"I don't think there's anything you can do to freak her out. I'm not going to reveal what she fantasizes about, but trust me on this one, Terry."

"Fantasizes? My wife doesn't fantasize."

"Fuck you your wife doesn't fantasize. She cut you off sexually, do you think she cut herself off too? You'd be surprised at your wife's arsenal of self-pleasuring devices."

"My wife has sex toys? I've never seen them."

"Honey, men don't hold the monopoly on masturbation."

"Well, how do I go from being who I am to who she wants me to be in the bedroom?"

"It's true you are Clark Kent-ish, but I know that Superman is hiding just below the surface and I'm going to help him come out."

My eyes lit up.

"Now don't get the wrong idea, Terry, I may be polyamorous, but I'm not about to fuck my best friend's husband. However, I am going to give you and her the best gift I can. I'm going to teach you how to fuck your wife the way she wants it. Now listen up because Alpha School is in session."

CHAPTER NINETEEN

All Apologies

I had finally drifted off to sleep around four in the morning but was awoken shortly thereafter by the sound of a car door opening and closing. A moment later, Terry was standing in our bedroom; he looked disheveled and held a black marble composition book in his hands.

The shame I felt at what I'd done earlier, in our own home nonetheless, made it hard for me to maintain eye contact with him. I tugged our bedsheets up as I didn't want to expose myself to him as I was sleeping in the nude.

"Look, Terry, last night," I started to say, but he cut me off.

"Be quiet," he said to me. "There's something I need to tell you."

He remained in the doorway, opened the notebook he carried with him, and read to me the journal entry he wrote after we made love for the first time. If that caught me completely off guard, what he said next stunned me.

"I broke the promise I made to myself that night. I

became someone who I'm not proud of, someone who put his ambition ahead of the love he has for his wife. For all of that, I ask for your forgiveness."

He was asking me for forgiveness? He walks in on me straddling another man and he's the one saying sorry? I was caught so off guard that I couldn't even reply.

"There's more. I was offered a partnership in the firm today, and I turned it down."

He then went on to tell me the great awakening he had in Florida and how he tried like hell to get home as early as he could last night. I was floored.

"Libby, can you forgive me for the way I've been acting towards you over the past fifteen years?"

I felt a heaviness in the pit of my stomach and couldn't stop my eyes from welling up with tears. "Yes," I said and then removed the covers and rushed towards him.

I placed my arms around his neck and drew his face into mine, not bothered by the scratchiness of his day-old stubble. He held on to me very tightly and I didn't want to break his embrace, but there were some things I had to say to him as well. I let go of my grasp and walked backward towards the bed and sat down. I motioned for him to sit next to me, but he remained standing.

"I've been feeling abandoned by you, so last night, when you didn't show up for the exhibition, I decided to take my anger out on you by seducing my trainer."

"Libby, you don't have to…"

She cut me off, "Yes, I do."

I then explained what happened, and importantly what didn't happen, with Jack. I told him about my near miss in the past but reinforced how much I loved him and once again asked for his forgiveness.

"I forgive you, Libby."

Hearing those four words were like having shackles undone and being freed from the chains that had been binding me for years.

"Do you think we can start over, Terry? Do you think we can bury our old marriage tonight and have it start anew?"

I wanted nothing more than to put the past behind us and rush towards my new future with my husband.

"Yes, Libby, I think we can do that, but it's important for you to know that there's another way in which I have changed."

"I'm not sure I know what you mean."

"You will. Stand up."

Did he just tell me to stand up? Giving commands was very uncharacteristic of Terry. I stood up, unsure of what was happening.

"I want you to take my shirt off, Libby."

Take his shirt off? Who is this man and what has he done with my normally docile husband? I walked up to him and slowly unbuttoned his shirt, starting at his neck and ending with the button at his waist. I pulled it off his shoulders and the entire time we never broke eye contact.

"And my undershirt," he said.

I bit my lip with excitement. He'd never been so commanding before, and I eagerly tugged his shirt over his head.

"I want you to look at my body, Libby. Do you like it?"

My husband always kept himself in good shape and it had been a while since I'd given a long, hard look at his body. I certainly liked what I saw. "Yes," I said and then reached out to touch him, but he swatted my hand away.

"No touching for now," he said and then gave me one of those trademark Terry smirks. Simply because I couldn't touch him made me want to feel his body that much more—and feel it pressed against mine.

"You don't get to have it tonight. No, tonight we are just going to lie in bed together and hold each other until we fall asleep."

"But Terry, I want to…"

"This is not about what you want, Libby, it's about what I want and tonight I just want to hold you until we fall asleep."

I was shocked. My husband, who I hadn't offered myself to in over three months, was saying no to sex. This was certainly different, and I didn't know what to think about it.

"Are you sure…"

"We are not going to have sex tonight. Maybe we will tomorrow, I'm not sure, but when I'm ready, you'll know."

When he's ready? What about when I'm ready? I was ready right then and there!

I watched with longing as Terry slid out of his pants and then got into bed.

"Come to bed now, Libby."

I didn't know what to think but did what I was told and got into bed, facing my husband.

"Turn around and face the other way," he said. Once I did, I felt his body press up against mine. It has been so long since our bodies had been this close, it felt so good, so comfortable.

He pulled me in close and told me to match his breathing. He then took a few deep breaths, and I did so as well. After a while of breathing in unison, sleep came over us and we drifted off together.

The next morning I woke up and wondered if it was all a dream—did my husband and I have a heart-to-heart, accept each other's apologies, and then just fall asleep? I turned around and there was no sign of him and thought that I'd imagined it, but the smell of coffee wafting up from downstairs confirmed that I wasn't alone in the house.

I got up, wrapped my robe around me, and followed the aroma downstairs and found my husband struggling to get a bagel out of the toaster.

"Need some help with that?"

My husband turned around and I saw that he was holding a knife in his hand. "I made you a bagel, but it's stuck in the toaster. I was using this to pry it out."

I took the knife from his hand and put it on the counter and then hugged Terry.

"Don't worry about the bagel," I said. "Let's go upstairs."

He slid his hands down my back until they rested on my bottom and then gave it a gentle squeeze. "Not yet," he whispered into my ear.

The Terry of the past few years was a man who had no self-discipline when it came to sex—all I had to do was suggest the possibility of making love and his pants would fly off. Now, in his place, was a guy who seemed completely in control of his desires—it made me wonder, is he still hungry for me and, if not, was it because he found satisfaction somewhere else? Something was definitely different about him.

"Are you opening the gallery today?" he asked, reminding me that I actually did have to work that Friday.

I needed to pack up each of the pieces that sold last night, load them into our delivery van, and deliver them to the winners.

"Shit," I said, looking at my watch, "I need to be there in thirty minutes. What are your plans?"

"Well, I called the firm's HR department this morning and explained I needed to take a few days off as I'm just not ready to deal with the repercussions from yesterday just yet."

That got me thinking, what was he going to do for work? I couldn't imagine him staying at the firm after he turned down his partnership, which made me wonder what his plan was. This was so Lloyd Dobler of him.

"What are you going to do…"

Terry put a finger to my mouth. "I don't know yet," he said. "But I'm never going back to the way I was."

This was both comforting and scary to me at the same time. While I appreciated knowing he was going to put me first, I had to admit I was a little uneasy about what the future would hold.

"I'll give you a ride to the gallery," he said. "Then I'm going to an afternoon meeting."

"For work?" I asked. I was confused given his state of employment was questionable.

"No. A personal meeting, I've taken on a mentor," he replied.

Mentor? Terry wasn't exactly the personal development type. What could he possibly want from a mentor?

"Does this new mentor have a name?" I asked.

For the second time that morning he put a finger to my lips. "In time, I will tell you everything. For now, it's time that you got ready for work."

Why was he being so vague? What spell had been cast over my husband and by what witch? I didn't know if I should hate her or thank her.

I was about to ask another question, but his stare suggested our chat was over. I left my husband in the kitchen and went upstairs to prepare for my day.

CHAPTER TWENTY

Alpha School

Terry dropped me off at the gallery and then went off to his mystery lunch. I told him I'd likely be doing deliveries all afternoon and wouldn't feel like cooking when I got home. We decided to go out to dinner at our favorite Mexican place, Tequila Mockingbird, just a few towns over in New Canaan.

My day went by in a flash given I was busy packing up all the paintings that had been purchased the night before and then hand delivered them all over Westport. I returned to the gallery in the middle of the afternoon to reload my delivery van and saw Terry's car parked on Main Street—it wasn't far from my gallery and I wondered if he was still meeting with his mentor. He didn't tell me where they were going to be meeting, but seeing that his car was on Main Street, I assumed he was having an extended lunch with this mystery mentor somewhere nearby.

I still had another round of deliveries to make and didn't dwell on it anymore as I was eager to get home, change, and have a nice dinner with Terry. Had I known who this mentor was, and where he was meeting her, I'd have gone nuclear on them both, but I didn't at the time —that detonation would come later. Now, it's time to see what went down from Terry's perspective.

#

I watched from a distance as Libby's delivery van took a left turn on Main Street, and then crossed the road and went to Marley's apartment. After she buzzed me in I walked up the stairs to her door, eager to have my second lesson.

She was dressed in jeans and a white blouse—both were very flattering to her figure. Her red hair looked radiant in the sunlight that came through her window and I could see why guys would line up to spend time with her—she wasn't just beautiful, she was hot and radiated sexuality. Though I wasn't there to be dominated by Marley, I was there to learn from her.

"Please tell me you didn't give in and fuck her last night," Marley said.

"She wanted to, but I held back with every fiber of my being."

"Good," Marley said. "Like all of us, subs enjoy sex, but they also get off on having someone else be in control of the experience. Your withholding from her likely drove her crazy, which is a good thing. Let pressure build under the volcano and then enjoy the eruption."

"I'm a little nervous about some of the things you told me I needed to do in order to dial up my alpha qualities," I said. It's true, I wasn't confident about being so forceful in the bedroom, thinking that it might backfire.

"Then that's what we are going to work on this

afternoon," she said.

"But how are we going to do that?" I asked. "It's not like Libby is here."

"We are going to do some role-playing, Terry Gardner. Don't worry, I don't bite. Well, that's a lie. I sometimes bite, but I won't bite you."

Role-playing? What did she mean by role-playing?

"How does your lovemaking typically start?"

"Well, I typically beg Libby for sex and then we get into bed."

Marley shook her head. "You are an alpha now. From here on out, you will not be asking her for sex."

"What, am I just supposed to tell her and expect her to give in every time?"

Smack! She hit me with the riding crop again. Where the hell does she hide that thing so that it is always in arm's reach but yet always unseen?

"No, that's what assholes do. When you want sex, you will go up to your wife, pull her close, and whisper into her ear the following phrase. 'I want me inside you.' That way, you are telling her what you want but not what she has to do."

There was something so erotic about being taught how to be alpha by an alluring redhead who knows you are off limits. *Or did she?*

"Try it on me."

"Okay…"

"Wait, we need to make this more real. Set the stage for me. Where would this happen, in the kitchen? In the bedroom? In the bathroom before a shower?"

I thought about when my desire for sex is at its highest and it is typically when I see my wife with nothing but a towel on as she is about to get into the shower.

"Bathroom," I said. "Just before she gets into the shower."

"Follow me."

I followed Marley to the bathroom, where she stood in front of the mirror pretending to look at herself— thankfully she didn't strip down into a towel as I'm not sure I could have handled that.

"I'm ready when you are, Terry."

"Okay," I said and then coughed to clear my throat. "I want me inside of you."

"No, no, no. You can't say it while you are standing in the doorway. You've got to push yourself against her and pin her against the counter to restrict her movement. As a sub, it will be a sign that you are taking control and she'll like it. Trust me. Try it again."

I walked into the bathroom and stared at Marley, contemplating what I was about to do.

"Are you waiting for a director to call action? Let's get on with it!"

I leaned forward and put my mouth to Marley's ear, "I want me inside you."

"Take a cold shower, buddy," she replied while turning around and slapping me. "What did I say about pinning her against the counter? Push yourself into her. Make Libby feel your package against that tight little ass of hers. Again!"

Marley turned around and mimed doing her makeup again. I took a deep breath to prepare for my third take, rehearsed what I was about to do in my mind, and after the imaginary director in my head shouted "Action" I pushed my pelvis into Marley's backside, leaned into it so that she could feel the bulge in my pants against her jeans, and grunted, "I want me inside you," into her ear.

She didn't turn around nor did she stop me. She simply pushed herself into me and started grinding.

"Well done, Terry Gardner," she said.

I held myself against her and felt a change coming over me—a physical change. I was becoming aroused.

"Now that you've got that under your belt, let's talk about how you can be more alpha when you are in the act. Where do you typically fuck her?"

"In the bed," I replied.

"Only the bed?" she asked.

"Well, I'd love to do it somewhere else, but every time I've asked, Libby always sighs."

"That's because she wants you to be an alpha and alphas don't ask. But whatever, for the purposes of what we are going to do next, the bed is fine."

Marley got into her bed while I stood in the doorway of her bathroom.

"I know you are big, Terry, but you can't fuck her from the doorway if she's on the bed," Marley said while patting the mattress.

I walked nervously over to the bed.

"Now I know from Libby that you are purely a missionary man, but I'm guessing that's because you are too timid to tell her that you want something else. Am I right?"

I nodded.

"Am I also right to assume that your foreplay only consists of you giving her oral because you don't tell her what you want?"

"You are batting a thousand."

"Okay, first things first, know that Libby loves the way you go down on her, apparently you are very talented in that regard, so bravo, loverboy. Also know that she'd love to go down on you, but you are going to have to ask for it because she's just not going to do it."

"I don't understand women."

She smacked me again with the riding crop. I swear, she must have these hidden throughout her apartment.

"No, you don't understand subs."

"Yes, Goddess," I said sarcastically. Another slap.

"Concentrate. Alright, let's say you are going down on Libby in the bed and that you want her to go down on you before you penetrate her. How are you going to tell her?"

Marley lay on her back and parted her legs and then held out her hand and gave me the come-hither motion with her pointer finger.

I walked to the foot of her bed and positioned myself between Marley's legs—thank goodness those jeans were on because my engine was revving. I grabbed her hands and then put my face between her legs but was careful not to make contact with her jeans.

"You hold her hands while you do that?" Marley asked. She sounded surprised.

"Yes," I said. "Is that bad?"

"No, just surprising. It's kind of an alpha thing to do, to restrict her hand movements."

"She always liked it that way," I said.

"Makes sense. Alright, so you are going down on her, getting her all good and wet. When do you typically stop?"

"I stop just before I sense she's about to climax as I know she likes to come with me inside her."

"How do you know she's about to climax?"

"She squeezes my head with her thighs and starts rocking her hips up and down."

On cue, Marley squeezed her leg muscles and moaned, "Terry, put your cock inside me."

This caught me way off guard and I stopped.

"You can't stop, Terry, that will kill the mood. Let's try it again."

I resumed my position between her legs, she contracted them and repeated her line. I then slid up her body and replaced my face with my pelvis.

"What are you doing?" she asked.

"I'm pretending to penetrate you."

"Why?"

"Because you just said you wanted me inside you."

Marley exhaled loudly, clearly disappointed in me.

"Yes, but you want her to blow you, right? She can't blow you if you are fucking her."

"This is all very confusing," I admitted and then rolled off of her.

"No, Terry, it's not. You want her to suck your cock, she wants to suck your cock, but you have to tell her to. Remember, you have to think like an alpha. Let's try it again."

I scooted back down the bed and put my face between her legs once again. This time, though, I could feel heat radiate from her body and that started to drive me wild. She squeezed her thighs against my face again and told me she wanted me inside her. This time, I slid up and positioned myself on top of her, put my arms under her, and rolled around so that I was on my back and she was on top of me. "Not until you give me what I want." And then I push on her shoulders until she is eye level with the bulge that is pulsating under my jeans.

This sudden movement catches Marley off guard and speechless for a moment. "Fuck, Terry. That was good."

I could tell she was a bit dazed and couldn't help but think she might have been contemplating unzipping my pants and taking me into her mouth. *Slut (and I mean that lovingly).*

She shook her head a bit and brought herself back to reality.

"Now that we have that under our belt, there's one more thing we need to work on."

"What's that?"

"Getting beyond missionary. I personally love it, especially since it gives me great access to rub my clit while a guy is penetrating me, but since that's the only thing you guys do, we need to work on your transitioning skills."

"Transitioning skills?"

"Yeah. There are two parts you are going to have to work on: telling her what position you want to move to and getting into it without breaking your stride and killing momentum."

Marley got onto her back and spread her legs. By now I knew that I had to get on top of her as missionary position was going to be our starting point. After I was in position, I once again felt the heat from between her legs coming through her jeans and onto my bulge. This excited me and my arousal was quickly given away.

"Don't worry, cowboy, it happens all the time. Now, what position do you want to go into?"

"I've always wanted to try doggie-style, but she would never consider it."

"You would be driven mad if you only knew how many times she's told me she wanted you to take her from behind."

"Really?" I asked.

"Yeah, really. Our little Libby has got quite the imagination. Okay, from here your goal is to get her into doggie-style. Give it a try."

I rested my body on top of hers and then whispered into her ear, "Let's try doggie."

"No!" she said loudly. "First, you made it sound like an option and second, don't say doggie. That might kill the mood if she starts thinking about puppies. Try again."

I got back into position, but this time Marley raised her legs up just a bit and crossed them behind my back, and I grew more aroused. I leaned into her ear and said, "I want to fuck you from behind."

"Better," she said. "You are focusing on what you want, but now that she's already let you in, what Libby as a sub really wants is for you to tell her what to do. Keep that in mind and try it again."

Marley wrapped her legs around me again and then bit her lip when my arousal pressed against her. If I didn't know any better, I'd have assumed she was getting off on this. I leaned into her ear and whispered, "Turn around."

"Oh yeah, stud, that's it. You gave her a command and told her exactly what you wanted. Now we have to work on the transition. To make it seamless, raise your hips so that you slide out, rest yourself on your knees, and then grab my hips and spin me around. Then push yourself into me.

I got back into position once again and mimed sliding out of Marley. I placed my feet under my butt so that I was sitting seiza, and then grabbed her hips and turned her around. She was now on all fours and I was staring at one of the most heavenly asses I've ever seen.

"I think you are forgetting something," Marley said, taking me out of my daze.

I positioned myself behind her and leaned my pelvis against her backside. She pushed into it and my arousal bulged between her cheeks.

"I think you've got it," she said.

"Now, this position gives you a wonderful opportunity to go really deep into her, which will drive her crazy. It also provides you the opportunity to play with her clit, which she calls her pearl."

"She does?"

"The fact that I know this and you don't speaks volumes. Now, push yourself against me and grab me by the hips."

I did as she commanded.

"Great," she said and then pushed up against my arousal. Now, are you right-handed or left?"

"Right," I said.

"Okay, take your right hand and slide it from my right hip down to the front of my body and pretend that I'm Libby and you want to rub my pearl."

I moved my hand so that it rested on Marley's stomach but was hesitant to move it between her legs. She grew impatient with me and then took my hand in hers and pushed it downward.

"Now you are going to want to rub it gently and in a circular motion. While you do that, slide in and out of her. If you can tell she's about to climax, push as deep as you can inside and then use two of your fingers to rub Libby's pearl. She'll feel as if she's died and gone to heaven.

By this point, I was so sexually charged that I felt as if I needed to leave Marley's bedroom and take a cold shower.

"I think that's enough for today's lesson," she said.

Thank God, I thought to myself. I looked at my watch and saw that it was now close to five o'clock and that I should get home to get ready for the first date I was going to have with my wife in about six months. As I was about to say my goodbyes to Marley, her buzzer rang announcing she had a visitor.

"Who is it?" Marley asked into her intercom.

"It's Libby," a voice came out of the speaker. "Can I come up?"

Marley saw the blood drain from my face. If Libby caught me here, she'd have a conniption, but I couldn't just leave and risk her seeing me in the hallway.

"Hide in the closet," she said and then walked to the intercom.

"Come on up," she said and pushed the button unlocking the door below.

CHAPTER TWENTY-ONE
Making Amends

I was done with my deliveries a little past four o'clock that afternoon and parked the van behind my gallery. I was about to go back home to prepare for my date with Terry, but thought about Marley and how uncomfortable I was about how things were between us. She was my closest friend in the world and lately it seemed as if we just hadn't been connecting. I was eager to tell her about Terry's change of heart and also address the wedge that had been driven between us lately. Since she only lived a block away from my gallery, and I knew she always worked from home on Fridays when she wasn't traveling, I decided to pay her a visit.

As I walked up Main Street, I was surprised to see Terry's car still parked where it was a few hours ago. Who was this mentor and what could they possibly have been talking about all this time? I made a mental note to ask him when we were out at dinner.

I pushed the button next to Marley's name to announce I was there.

"Who is it?" Marley asked.

"It's Libby," I replied. "Can I come up?"

A moment later I heard a buzz coming out of the door telling me it was unlocked. Soon after I was walking through Marley's door.

"Hey, chica," she said and gave me a hug.

She looked a little off—her white blouse appeared to be wrinkled and her normally pin-straight red hair looked disheveled. If I didn't know any better, I'd say she had been making out with someone.

"We have a lot to catch up on," I said.

"Since last night?" she asked.

I told her all about Jack turning out to be gay, Terry walking in on us, and then Terry's return home early that morning.

"You could get a book out of that, chica," she said.

"Maybe Terry could write it, given he's leaving the legal field."

"Really?" Marley said.

I then told her all about the talk Terry and I had after he returned. "And get this," I added, "he turned me down for sex last night. Should I be worried about that?"

The thought that he might be having an affair had crossed my mind a few times that day—that would certainly explain how he was so controlled around me earlier that morning.

"Give him time, chica," Marley said. "You two have been through a lot over the past twenty-four hours. When he's ready, I'm sure he'll let you know."

"I'm just not used to him having that kind of control over me. I've been thinking about fucking him all day— maybe it's because he wouldn't let me."

"Or he's giving you a taste of your own medicine."

I know she didn't mean that maliciously, but it stung nonetheless.

"There's another thing that's bugging me," I said. "Terry told me this morning that he hired a mentor and that they were meeting for lunch. His car has been parked in the same spot all day. That's a long lunch."

"What kind of mentor?" she asked.

"When I asked he just gave me a really vague answer like, 'in time I'll let you know,' or something like that. I know this sounds crazy, but do you think he could be having an affair?"

"You said it yourself, chica, that he didn't have the guts to cheat."

"I know, but between him turning me down for sex and now this mystery mentor, I'm a bit more suspicious."

"That man loves you, Libby, just be patient and it will be alright."

This was a far cry from the doom and gloom Marley of the prior Sunday as well as the stand-up comedian Marley that following Tuesday. Something was off.

"Are we okay?" Marley asked.

I loved this woman like a sister and I know that all relationships have ups and downs, but I needed to confront her on one last thing—whether or not she had a thing for my husband. She admitted as much at the Duck on Sunday and then there was her stand-up routine where she talked about never letting his penis leave her sight. I wanted to make it crystal clear that he was off limits to her.

"Do you have feelings for my husband?" I asked.

She had a hard time maintaining eye contact.

"What would make you think that?" she asked.

"I see the way you look at him," I said. "And then there's those jokes you told Tuesday night. Look, I know we have all known each other a very long time and that Terry and I have gone through a rough patch recently, but I am intent on making this work with him and I want to be sure you understand that."

"I'm a little insulted that you would even think I'd make a play for Terry. He's like the brother I never had."

She seemed sincere.

"Then yes, we are okay. Want to do drinks this Sunday?"

"The Duck again?"

"No," I said. "Let's treat ourselves to someplace classy. How about that place Longshore?"

Longshore was an outdoor bar overlooking Long Island Sound that was popular with Westport's well-to-do citizens.

"It's a plan."

I got up to leave in order to get ready for my date with Terry when I remembered that the little black dress I wanted to wear that night was still at the dry cleaner and I didn't have enough time to pick it up. Since it was going to be our first date in a long time, I wanted to look sexy for my husband and I knew that Libby had no lack of sexy options in her closet.

"Oh, do you have a little dress I can borrow for tonight? Mine's at the cleaners and I want to bring my A-game for Terry."

I saw the expression on her face change immediately. "Dress?" she asked.

"Something that will get his motor running so we do

more than just hug goodnight tonight. Can I just go in and pick something out?"

"The thing is," Marley said, "I've got company in the bedroom at the moment."

"Oh," I said, surprised that she had taken a lover in the middle of the afternoon dressed as she was. "Are you in a Dom session or something, because you look a little overdressed."

"You could say I'm training him."

"He's been awfully quiet since I got here," I said—there was something suspicious about this. Was there another reason she didn't want me in her room?

"He's very well aware that he'll get punished if he speaks up," Marley replied. "Comes with the territory of being my sub. Let me run in and get something for you," she said.

"That would be great," I replied.

I remained in her living room when she darted into the bedroom to grab a dress. I heard some hushed words exchanged and Marley came back a moment later with two dresses for me to consider: one black and one red. As I took them from her, my phone buzzed—it was a text from Terry.

T: I can't wait to see you tonight.

L: Where are you?

T: Finishing up with my mentor. Home in twenty. Care for a shower?

L: Yummy.

"That was Terry," I said. "I have to go."

"Have fun tonight, chica."

We hugged goodbye and I left her place to go back home. I thought about waiting at Terry's car to surprise him but was eager to get home and maybe steal a quick catnap before getting ready for dinner—maybe even followed by some private time in the shower with Terry.

CHAPTER TWENTY-TWO

A Misunderstanding

I went right upstairs and reclined on my bed after succumbing to the exhaustion that built up after such a crazy week. I only woke up when I sensed that Terry was hovering over me—I imagined him undressing me with his eyes.

"Hello stranger, how was your meeting with the mystery mentor?"

"I intend to tell you all about it," he said teasingly while brushing the hair out of my eyes. "But not right now. Right now, we have to take a shower."

That sounded heavenly. I offered my arms to Terry and he took them and pulled me out of the bed and led me to our bathroom, where he started the water to the shower. I glanced at the bathtub I used on Sunday morning and secretly wished we were taking a bath instead.

I started to unbutton my blouse, but Terry came up from behind me and whispered, "Let me do that," into my ear. He then ran his strong hands up my body and grazed my breasts before undoing each of my buttons slowly, sensuously.

When there were no buttons left, he untucked my blouse and pulled it off me. My bra was next, and he had no trouble undoing the front snaps—how much he had learned since our college days. I took his hands in mine and slid them upwards towards my breasts, which were extra sensitive—I missed his touch so much it was driving me wild.

I looked in the mirror and saw that smirk on his face that I'd fallen in love with twenty years ago. He then slid his hands gently down my body and unbuttoned, and then unzipped, my jeans. He knelt down behind me to remove them and then nibbled on my cheeks before coming back up.

"We've got a problem, Terry Gardner," I said. "You still have your clothes on."

I then spun around so that our chests were touching and started to unbutton his shirt.

"No," he said and pushed my hands to my sides. "You are not allowed to touch me until after dinner."

Where was this coming from and why was he doing this to me? I wanted to touch my husband, I needed to touch my husband and he wouldn't let me. Never in our twenty years of couplehood had he denied me like this. I was suspicious about this change in Terry's behavior but was also incredibly turned on by his taking a dominant role in our physicality.

I watched him remove his shirt and jeans and stared with longing as he removed his briefs and freed that object I first laid eyes on twenty years ago when he was the nude model for my figure drawing class. It had been so long since he'd been inside me, and so much of that was my own doing, that I found I had a craving for it.

"You can look, but you can't touch," Terry said, sensing where my mind had gone. Did he know how much he was driving me wild?

He opened the door to the shower for me and motioned that I should get inside. As the hot water covered my body, I felt my muscles start to relax. I reached for the poof I kept in the shower so that I could douse it in body wash, but once again my hands were swept away. "I will bathe you," he whispered into my ear while pressing his body against mine. "Turn around," he said, and I did as instructed so that my back was against his chest.

As he moved to grab the body wash, I could feel that beautiful specimen attached between his legs graze my backside and it took every ounce of strength I had not to reach around and grab it with my hand and guide it to where I needed it to be.

He started massaging my stomach with the poof until it was slick with a foamy lather. He worked his hand upward until the spongy appendage he held cleaned my breasts, arms and neck. Being pampered like this, without the expectation of reciprocation, was turning me on in a way that I hadn't anticipated. It was like someone taught him how to seduce me the way I had longed for.

"Push up against the wall and spread your hands and legs."

Was he bathing me or about to frisk me? I did as he instructed and felt the sponge caress my neck and back. When those were done, I sensed him kneel down behind me to bathe my legs—he started at the ankles and worked his way up to my calves and then thighs. He paused before reaching my backside and then repeated with the opposite leg, just grazing the spot between my legs that was aching for him to penetrate.

While he was still bending down behind me, I felt him reach for the bottle of body wash again, but this time instead of putting it on the poof, he applied it to his hands. He then proceeded to rub my ass, taking care to make sure I was clean all over.

I was full of anticipation and longed for him to reach those strong hands to the triangle between my legs and feel how excited he was making me. Instead, he stood up and grabbed the detachable shower head and rinsed me off. As the pulsating jets of warm water went over my backside and splashed between my legs, it took all my strength to hold myself back from grabbing the shower head and finishing myself off.

I then watched as he lathered up his own body and rinsed off. I wanted nothing more than to do that for him, but he had been clear that I wasn't allowed to touch him until given permission, and permission had yet to be granted.

"Good things come to those who wait," he said and then turned the water off, signaling that shower time was over. He helped me dry off and I hoped I could return the favor, but he took care of that himself.

"I'm going to get dressed," he whispered into my ear. "I assume you have to do some girly stuff in here, so I'll leave you be."

"Okay," I said with a frown.

"Patience, my dear, I'll give you what you want after dinner."

The way he was acting and how he was talking were driving me crazy inside. I didn't want to wait until after dinner, but what choice did I have?

I did my hair and makeup while he got dressed. When I was done, I saw the pile of clothes on the bathroom floor and considered leaving them there for later but decided to pick them up and bring them to our hamper.

Our discarded clothing was all mixed together and when I picked everything up I noticed that there was a single long red hair on his shirt—it looked like one of Marley's. At the time I assumed it had attached to something I was wearing when I hugged her earlier in the day and transferred to his shirt when our clothes wound up in a pile on the floor. I didn't think anything more of it.

Once I was ready, we went to the restaurant and our date was going great. We each had one of the restaurant's signature margaritas and got caught up on the events of the past week—I told him all about the art exhibition and he gave me the full story about his time in Florida, including the time he spent with the eccentric owner of his firm, his reuniting with his siblings, and his father's illness. This last part saddened me as I adored Gerry.

"You should go back down there. Actually, why don't we both go and spend some time with him?"

"We certainly could use the time away, and I'm going to have some free time on my hands. Let's do it!" he said and then took out his phone.

"What are you doing?"

"Booking a weekend trip to Fort Lauderdale, just wait until you experience Yasgur's Farm South."

My Lloyd Dobler was back. Lawyer Terry would never agree to doing something spur of the moment, but the old Terry—the guy I fell in love with—wouldn't think twice about throwing caution to the wind and whisking me away on a weekend adventure.

"Done," he said. "JetBlue out of Westchester tomorrow morning."

"You work fast, Terry Gardner," I said.

"Not all the time," he whispered into my ear.

That intimate moment was interrupted by the hostess who came over to tell us that our table was ready. Once we sat down, we ordered two more drinks and resumed our conversation.

"So what's your plan?" I asked casually. While I was happy he was leaving the legal profession, I was eager to know what he planned to do for work. We certainly couldn't afford to maintain our lifestyle on my income from the gallery.

"I'm thinking about writing again," he said. "I have this great idea for a novel."

"Really," I said and leaned across the table. "Give it to me."

He winked at me to acknowledge my choice of words and leaned in closer like I'd done.

"It's about this married couple who hits a rough patch, but true love prevails and they live happily ever after."

"Sounds familiar," I said.

"Now dis is what I love to see," a booming voice said from across the room. It was Hugo, the head waiter at Tequila Mockingbird, who always has a way of inserting himself into our conversations at the most inopportune times. Even though he's lived in the United States for almost thirty years, his Colombian accent is still very thick and we have a hard time understanding him at times.

"A jung couple in love make my heart sing." He played air guitar as he said this.

"How have you been, Hugo?" Terry said. I offered my husband a concerned look out of fear that this would encourage a lengthy exchange.

"Ju two have no been here een a while. Where ju been?"

"It's all my fault," Terry said. "Too much work and not enough play."

"Tary, ju canno let such a beautiful woman like Meez Libby here alone too long. You must romance the pant off of her."

Damn right, I thought to myself. I certainly want the pants romanced off of me after dinner.

"I'm a new man now, Hugo. This woman, for now and forever, will be at the center of my world."

"So goo to see Meester Tary. Let me take a picture of ju two birds of luv."

I grabbed my phone but saw that it was no longer on. "My phone is dead, Terry give him yours."

Terry handed Hugo his phone and, since we were sitting across from each other, we both leaned in and smiled at Hugo, who snapped no fewer than fifteen pictures.

"Lemme jus make sure dat there's a good one in dere."

"Hugo, that's really not necessary," Terry said while getting up to take his phone back, as if there was something on it he didn't want Hugo to see.

"No a problem," Hugo said as he scrolled through the pictures. A second later his eyes grew wide. "Ay caramba, pene grande."

"What does that mean?" I asked.

"It's nothing," I said.

"Oh Meez Libby, I'm not sure if I happy for ju or

worried for ju," Hugo said and then laughed. "I go and get you guacamole. Dat one will be on me."

Hugo walked away shaking his head and laughing—I looked at my husband.

"What was that all about? What could he possibly see on your phone that led to that kind of reaction?"

I could see the blood drain from Terry's face and then he took a deep breath.

"Well, in the spirit of being completely honest with each other, he just saw this."

Terry handed me his phone and I gasped when I looked at the screen. "Why the hell do you have a picture of your dick on your phone?"

He then told me about his father's friend Sol and the advice he was given.

"An old Jewish guy who teaches retired people all about tantra tells you to send me a dick pic and you went as far as to take it."

"Yep," Terry said. "That's pretty much it."

I started to laugh at the absurdity of it all. "Well, thank God you didn't send it. I'm not sure what I would have done."

I knew when Terry broke eye contact and looked at the floor that something was wrong.

"Wait, what?" I asked. "You didn't send it, right? If you did, I certainly didn't see it."

"About that," he said. "This is kind of funny, but I accidentally sent it to someone else."

I could tell he was nervous, but needed to know who the recipient of my husband's dick pic was.

"Who?" I asked.

"It's not important," he replied.

"Who?" I pressed.

"Marley," he said. "I accidentally sent it to Marley."

I immediately went numb. Marley, my best friend, who I assumed had been obsessing over Terry's penis had received a picture of it and didn't tell me.

I put my drink down, stared at Terry in the eyes, and went strictly business on him.

"Walk me through just exactly how that happened."

Terry told me about how Marley had reached out to him to talk the night before he sent the picture and how he was involved in a text exchange with her right before he was going to send me the picture.

"Look, it was an accident," he said. "I apologized to her and tried to forget it."

I couldn't believe this. "Let me see the exchange."

"Libby, come on. That's not necessary."

"Give me your phone, Terry."

He reluctantly handed his phone over and I scrolled through it to find their correspondence.

"It's about time you came to your senses, Terry…show me the head, Terry," I said, quoting the exchange. When I got to the point where she said he had some hard lessons to learn, it was like a lightbulb went on over my head. A vision of his car parked near her apartment all day came into my head and then there was the rogue red hair I found in the pile of clothes on the floor.

"Is Marley your so-called mentor?" I asked.

"It's not what you think…"

"Were you at her place this afternoon?" I asked with a raised voice.

"Libby, please, don't raise your voice. I can explain everything, just give me a moment."

So that was it, he had been with Marley, my sexually dominant friend. No wonder he didn't want to fuck me when I offered myself to him—he was probably wiped out in that department.

"Don't even bother," I said and then got up and started to walk out of the restaurant just as Hugo was coming back with the guacamole.

"Where ju going, Meez Libby?"

I ignored his question and stormed out of the restaurant.

CHAPTER TWENTY-THREE

The End of the Innocence

After I left the restaurant, I drove like a woman possessed over to Marley's place and prayed that she was home so that I could tear her a new one. Terry tried calling multiple times, but I ignored him.

After pushing the button to announce my arrival, I heard Marley's voice come out of the speaker, "Who is it?" she asked.

"We need to talk, now," I said angrily into the intercom. When the buzzer sounded, I pushed the door open, charged up the stairs, and pounded on her door. She opened it and I bolted inside.

"How long have you been fucking my husband?"

"Excuse me?" Marley replied.

"I saw your little text exchange, Marley," I said. "And I know he was here earlier today."

"And so he told you what we were doing?" Marley said.

"He didn't need to tell me. I'm not a fucking idiot, I know how you are with men."

"Really," she said.

"Yes, really. I know how you dominate them and what you do to them in the bedroom. It's no wonder he hasn't wanted to fuck me since he's been home, because he's been fucking you and you fucked all the fuck out of him."

In my mind, that was a world record for the use of the word fuck and its derivatives in a sentence.

"Fuck you, Libby, if you think I would fuck my best friend's husband."

"So you deny it?"

Before she could respond, her buzzer rang.

"Don't you dare answer that," I said.

"You don't tell me what to do in my home," she replied and then impatiently asked, "Who is it?" into the intercom.

"It's Terry," a frantic voice said. "Is Libby there?"

He must have taken an Uber over to Marley's place as I sped off with his car.

"I don't want to see him," I replied.

"It's my place and my call," Marley said and then spoke into the intercom, "Come on up."

Terry entered Marley's apartment just a few seconds later and looked out of breath given his sprint up the stairs and down the hall.

"Forget your underwear or something?" I said.

"There's a very reasonable explanation for all of this," he said. "If you just allow me to…"

I raised my hand to his face and said, "Shut the fuck up, Terry."

"Terry," Marley said. "Remember, an alpha doesn't ask someone to listen, he tells them to."

"What the fuck does that mean?" I asked.

"Listen to your husband, Libby."

Great, two against one. "I'm listening."

"Yes, I was here earlier and I was also here after walking in on you and your trainer Thursday night."

"What, for some revenge sex? How clichéd."

"Your friend over there cares about you more than you know," Terry said. "So much so that she offered to train me on how to be dominant in the bedroom."

"What the hell does that even mean?" I asked. Nothing made sense anymore.

"You've been complaining to me for years that Terry isn't aggressive enough for you and that he is too polite a lover. I offered to teach him how to give you what it is you want in the bedroom."

"And you did that by fucking him?"

"No," both Marley and Terry said in unison. "By training him. You want to know why he hasn't fucked you since he got home? It's because I told him not to, not because I wore him out. Believe me, if he was with me, there'd be scars. Have you seen any scratches or black and blue marks on his body?"

"No," I said. "But that doesn't mean anything."

"Libby," Terry said. "I swear to God nothing happened between us, all she did was teach me how I should act towards you sexually."

"Well, you haven't acted towards me sexually at all, so I guess she didn't teach you that much."

"That's not true. Remember the shower we took right before coming to dinner?"

"The shower where all you did was tease me?"

"Yes. Who was in control?"

"You were, but…"

Terry cut me off. "Think about all the times we've been

in similar situations. What happened?"

"We had sex."

"Would I have ever told you not to touch me?"

"No," I admitted.

"The first thing Marley taught me was to withhold myself from you in order to build anticipation. Did it work?"

I thought about just lying in bed with him the night before, how I felt in the morning when I wanted to have sex with him and he said no, and the longing I felt during—and ever since—our shower together. "Yes," I admitted.

"Terry," Marley said. "I think it's time to show her all I've taught you."

After she said this, Marley started walking towards the door.

"Where are you going?" I asked.

"Out," she replied. "It's time for my student to practice all he's learned."

She walked out the door and left us alone in her apartment. I turned around and looked at my husband.

"You don't expect me to believe any of this, do you?"

I expected him to put up a defense. Instead he said, "The only thing I expect right now is to give you what you've been missing."

The intensity of how he said it took me by surprise.

"There's no way I'm…"

Terry approached me and placed a finger over my mouth to stop me from talking. "I didn't fuck Marley, Libby. I have no desire to fuck Marley. But I am going to fuck you."

As he said these words, something came over me. Maybe it was adrenaline that had been running through my system since leaving the restaurant, or the sexual charge in the atmosphere combined with the roller coaster of sexual emotions I'd been feeling since Terry got home, but I felt my defenses start to come down.

"Look at me in the eyes, Libby," Terry said. I complied.

"The only woman I want to be with is standing right in front of me," he said and then approached me. I tried to resist, but whatever had been coming over me had obliterated my defenses and I let him not only approach me but wrap his arms around me. I looked into his eyes and felt tears being born from mine. As one was falling down my cheek, he stopped it with his finger and wiped it away.

"What are we going to do about us, Terry?" I said and buried my face into his chest.

He didn't respond, he just held me tighter, and then surprised me when he spun me around and ran his hands up my body and cupped my breasts. He then put his mouth to my ear and grunted, "It's time you got what you want."

If the intensity with which he spoke made me excited, the kiss he planted on my neck put me into overdrive. He directed me into Marley's bedroom and pushed me onto the bed.

"Take off your top," he said. I just looked at him, never before did he tell me what to do like that, but I found myself unbuttoning my blouse. Before I knew it I was sitting bare chested in front of my husband. I anticipated that his next request would be for me to remove the jeans I'd worn to dinner and stood to tug them off.

"Did I say you could take those off?"

His tone made it clear that there was no room for

negotiation, so I stopped what I was doing.

"Good, now come here and kiss me, but don't touch me with your hands. As a matter of fact, hold them behind your back."

I reached behind my back before getting up to walk towards my husband and stood on my tiptoes to kiss him on the lips. When our mouths touched, they opened simultaneously and he thrust his tongue inside my mouth.

As my passion rose, the excitement I felt in the center of my body had started to travel below my waist and I could feel the area between my thighs was getting wet with excitement.

"You may use your hands to remove my pants," he said.

I could now feel my heart beating in my throat—this is what I had longed for, Terry to take charge and tell me what to do. I undid his belt slowly and then got down on my knees, waist high to him, and unbuttoned his pants. I then slowly undid his zipper, careful not to touch the bulge underneath for fear of being scolded as he hadn't given me permission to touch it yet.

Once his zipper was down, I tugged his jeans off and was surprised to find he wasn't wearing anything underneath. While he'd been acting calm, cool, and collected, I was now face to face with that one part of his anatomy that couldn't betray how turned on he was at that moment. I wanted so badly to touch it, to kiss it, to have it slide inside me and fill me up with his love, but I knew that this new Terry had to give me permission first.

"Do you like what you see, Libby?"

"Yes," I said while looking him in the eyes. There's something so raw about looking at a man square in the eyes while on your knees in front of him. The fire burning inside me was now roaring.

"Close your eyes," he commanded and I complied.

"Now open your mouth."

I did as he told me and waited patiently for him to caress my lips with his excitement. He held off for a moment, which felt more like an eternity, but soon his flesh grazed my lips. It reminded me of the tips of the strawberries he fed to me the night we first made love and I opened my mouth wider anticipating he'd want me to take all of him in.

"Just kiss the top," he said, and I complied.

In our twenty years as a couple, he never once told me to please him with my mouth. I assumed he just didn't like it, but now I understand that the old Terry was too polite to ask for what he really wanted.

I kissed the top and tasted the saltiness of the sticky essence that leaked out of his tip. I then slid my tongue down his shaft and massaged his base with it before slowly sliding up to the tip. Encouraged to continue by his moans of pleasure, I did this one more time—even lighter than the first time—and then opened my mouth wide to take him in. His knees trembled with pleasure as I took all of him in and then gave my mouth a rest. I looked him in the eyes the entire time.

"Stand up," he said, and I did as I was told. By now I was dripping with excitement, I longed to touch myself between my legs but knew I'd be reprimanded for it.

"Turn around," he commanded, and I did as I was told. I then heard him get down on his knees so he was eye level with my bottom. I felt his strong hands grab my cheeks and pull them forward. I wanted to be free from my jeans to show him how excited I was and, fortunately, Terry didn't make me wait long. He slid them down and lifted my feet up, one at a time, to remove them.

"Lie on the bed face down," he said. I did and then felt his body on top of mine, his excitement resting on my ass. If he tried to push inside me, I would have let him in without resistance—I was that aroused. He didn't though. Instead, he kissed my neck and nibbled my earlobe. When his tongue entered my ear, I let out a gasp of pleasure.

He then slid his tongue over to my neck and left a trail of kisses down my back until his mouth was resting just below my waist.

"Part your legs."

That was a command he didn't have to repeat. I felt his tongue slide from the base of my spine down to the heart of my femininity—the exhale of his warm breath mixing with my arousal was almost too much for me to handle. I needed him inside me. He must have sensed this because he stopped what he was doing and slid up my body, his arousal now resting just outside heaven's door, and his excitement was knocking. I reached around to grab his arousal, unafraid at whatever he might have to say about it, but he didn't interrupt.

With him balancing over my body, I guided him in and felt his entirety slide inside me and fill me up, my body offering no resistance; I couldn't help but gasp with pleasure. It had been so long since he had been inside me and I felt so good, so complete. I wanted him as deep as he could go and pushed myself up onto my arms and thrust my hips backwards to take even more of him in.

I sensed my excitement build and that I was approaching a climax. I pushed back hard into him too and feverishly ground against his base to hasten my orgasm and then released with a shudder, unable to support myself with my arms any longer and rested on the bed with Terry still hard as a rock inside me. I was glad this new Terry still adhered to the nice guys finish last principle.

"I want to look you in the eyes when I climax," he whispered into my ear.

Who was I to deny him? I turned on my back and he immediately grabbed my hands and put them over my head. "Hold on to the bedpost."

I wanted to wrap my arms around him and push him towards me but dared not do anything until he commanded me to.

With my hands on the post, he kissed my chest and took my breasts into his mouth, gently licking my nipples. As he switched between them, I felt a rush of excitement between my legs and knew that my arousal was climbing once again.

He must have sensed this as well because he started making his way towards my waist, kissing me lightly as he traveled downward. Terry sometimes liked to tease me before taking me into his mouth, but this time he went right for me, opening his mouth above my pearl and sucking me in. I squeezed the bedpost I'd been holding with both hands as I raised my hips upwards and he bathed me with his tongue. Did I just climax again so soon after his being inside me?

Terry knew what I'd done. "Not fair," he said.

I wanted so badly to pull his body on top of mine, but knew that I couldn't use my hands—luckily he sensed what I wanted and made his way back to my face.

"Guide me inside," he said, and I immediately reached

down between his legs and grabbed his arousal. Before guiding it in, I stroked it a bit to make him harder and then rested it on my opening, which was once again dripping with desire. He pushed in slowly as he got harder, and the intensity was so strong I scratched my nails down his back. This only served to drive him wild and his speed intensified.

"Tell me what you want, Libby."

His command reverberated in my ear and I didn't respond right away—the pleasure I was experiencing so strong that I could barely speak. The combination of the act itself and Terry's raw masculinity was overwhelming. What did I want? I wanted to come again, that much I knew, but I also wanted to feel Terry explode with pleasure inside me. I wanted to feel every pulse of his arousal release his warm seed deep within me.

"Tell me what you want, Libby," he grunted louder than before.

"I want you to fuck me," I replied. This dirty talk seemed to drive him wild. "Fuck me hard, Terry Gardner. Fuck me until you come deep inside me."

His speed quickened, and I raised my knees up so he could enter me deeper. He went from sliding in and out of me to pushing on my pelvis as deep as he could and grinding on top of me without breaking contact. I reached between his legs and used a finger to massage the smooth spot where the base of his manhood ended. This seemed to push him over the edge and I felt that unmistakable pulse start from deep down inside him.

As his arousal climaxed, I felt his hot essence rush into me—our bodily fluids joining together as evidence of our passion. We had come together, there was no doubt about that.

#

That lovemaking was unlike anything I'd ever experienced in my life. Put simply, it was euphoric, and just what I needed.

While I was initially upset that Marley, whom I assumed had feelings for my husband, would take him under her wing sexually, I had to admit doing so was very likely the greatest gift she could have ever given me.

We both drifted off into a deep sleep in Marley's place and when I awoke, I was surprised to see that I was alone. Happily, though, I saw him at Marley's desk capturing his thoughts down on some scrap paper he'd found—the same way he did after we made love for the first time.

Epilogue

I started this story by referencing a marriage that was dead and how Terry, Marley, and I all played a role in its demise and burial. I'm happy to report, though, that Terry and I are still together—yes, our marriage as we knew it was long gone, but in its place sprang a new life together—a life where we are both open and honest with what we want in our relationship.

If there's anything I want you to take away from my experience it's that marriages, like all human relationships, can be fragile and they can shatter if not reinforced. Both Terry and I almost threw our marriage away when things got rocky—we almost gave in to the temptations that life put in front of us. However, we were fortunate enough to have people in our lives who helped us see the value in what we had and encouraged us to be open and honest with each other about how we are feeling.

I suppose that's the entire point of this story—while it can be difficult and uncomfortable to address what's bothering us about a partner, it is something that must be done—provided of course that we value the relationship and want to preserve it.

I loved my husband but didn't love the way he was always putting his job before me. Therefore I used sex as a weapon and put a wedge between us that almost split us up permanently. Furthermore, I felt as if I didn't need to be open with Terry about what I wanted from him physically in our relationship and took for granted that he would just know.

Thank goodness we had people in our lives who cared about both of us and encouraged us to make changes for the better. For Terry this was his father Gerry and the founder of his former law firm, Paul Hewson, the eccentric millionaire who played Ghost of Christmas Past.

And then there's Marley, who played an important role for both of us. She opened my eyes to the risks I was taking by treating my husband the way I was and she opened Terry's eyes as to what I wanted from him. While I certainly didn't think it at the time, the resurrection of my marriage is due in no small part to her efforts.

Now that I've said my piece, I'll bring you up to date on things that have happened since last spring.

I'll admit that, a year ago, I was a little worried that Terry would regret turning down the partnership at his law firm, but that never came to pass. What he didn't regret, though, was returning to Florida to visit his father before he passed away.

After that night at Marley's place, we moved forward with our spur-of-the-moment plans to fly down to Florida and visit with Gerry. Not long after our arriving, he was admitted to the hospital with respiratory issues and he would never be released. He passed away on the hospice floor of Holy Cross Hospital in Fort Lauderdale just three days after we'd arrived. I could tell he was happy that

Terry and I had made amends and that Terry had been able to reconnect with him and the rest of the family.

If there was a silver lining that came out of Gerry's passing it was that Terry actually inherited quite a bit of money from his father's lottery winnings. This safety net allowed us to stay in our home and maintain our lifestyle as Terry transitioned from life as a highly paid attorney towards fulfilling his dreams as a writer.

He started off small, selling some freelance pieces to magazines and blogs and then gradually started writing longer-form stuff and built a little following as an independent author. He's been happier than I've seen him in a decade—following his passion in both his career and in our bedroom helped turn our lives around.

Which reminds me, there's something he and I have to talk about later today because there's some news I've been keeping to myself since I was late for my last period—our family of two is about to expand.

This work summarizes my account of all I have learned about myself during my time in PET. It will forever serve as a reminder of how I was last year when my marriage was about to fall apart and all the steps we've taken since to preserve our relationship. I hope it has, in some way, helped you understand how important openness and honesty are to any relationship and that you can adopt those principles into your life so that you too can save something worth fighting for. If you know of anyone who could benefit from this story, please pass it on.

—The New Libby Gardner, March 2017

Acknowledgements

The Event is a work of fiction, but many of the scenes in this novel have been inspired by my actual experiences (though I'm not telling which ones).

I hope you enjoyed reading this book as much as I've enjoyed writing it. To that end, I need to give credit where credit is due and thank Aquila Editing (www.aquilaediting) for their guidance in turning my manuscript into a novel. I highly recommend their editing services to anyone.

I also want to thank my dear friends Susan and Erin for taking the time to read early versions of this manuscript and providing feedback on the overall story as well as their thoughts on where it was too steamy (and where it wasn't steamy enough). Thank you, ladies!

To stay up to date with everything Tori Shannon, please visit www.torishannon.com and be sure to sign up for my mailing list, where you'll be the first to be in the know about new books (you haven't seen the last of Marley Carlin) as well as find out how you can get advanced reader copies. If you want to email me directly, feel free to reach out using news@torishannon.com.

Happy Reading!

***

—Tori Shannon, March 2018